'If you don't want a wedding ring, we can deal very well together.'

Roman put his hands on Claudia's shoulders, towering over her. 'You know what I want. Come to me, Gemini Girl. You won't regret it.'

It would be so easy for Claudia to say yes to everything he was asking of her. 'No, Roman, it wouldn't work. I don't fancy being anyone's mistress, any more than you fancy being a husband.'

WE HOPE you're enjoying our new addition to our Contemporary Romance series—stories which take a light-hearted look at the Zodiac and show that love can be written in the stars!

Every month you can get to know a different combination of star-crossed lovers, with one story that follows the fortunes of a hero or a heroine when they embark on the romance of a lifetime with somebody born under another sign of the Zodiac. This month features a sizzling love-affair between **GEMINI** and **SAGITTARIUS**.

To find out more fascinating facts about this month's featured star sign, turn to the back pages of this book. . .

ABOUT THIS MONTH'S AUTHOR

Liza Goodman says: 'Born on the 24th December, I am a Capricorn on the cusp of Sagittarius and I have the characteristics of both the determined, stable goat and the wide-roaming Archer, which can be confusing to other people. I am surrounded by Pisceans, my husband, one daughter and a son-in-law coming under that sign as did my sister and a cousin. My other daughters come under Leo and Taurus, and with the grandchildren I think we cover most of the other signs.'

GEMINI GIRL

BY

LIZA GOODMAN

MILLS & BOON LIMITED
ETON HOUSE   18–24 PARADISE ROAD
RICHMOND   SURREY   TW9 1SR

To my Granddaughter, Claudia Jackson, who has always shown a great interest in my writing and after whom my heroine is named.

First published in Great Britain 1992 by Mills & Boon Limited

© Liza Goodman 1992

Australian copyright 1992 Philippine copyright 1992 This edition 1992

ISBN 0 263 77547 X

STARSIGN ROMANCES is a trademark of Harlequin Enterprises B.V., Fribourg Branch. Mills and Boon is an authorised user.

Set in 10 on 12 pt Linotron Times 01-9205-50247 Z Typeset in Great Britain by Centracet, Cambridge Made and printed in Great Britain

CHAPTER ONE

SHE was floating along the aisle of a dimly lit church, the only reality the beautiful white dress she was wearing and the man waiting for her at the altar, and even he was shrouded in a mist, preventing her from seeing his face. Claudia quickened her steps; perhaps this time she would see him and know, at last, who he was, this man she would marry.

Bells rang out and she frowned; that was new—usually her dream was completely silent. The mist thickened, and the church and the man dissolved and disappeared, as they always did.

Claudia opened her eyes and blinked away the tears. It was foolish to cry for a dream but it was always so real, and knowing it was only her imagination didn't make it any less painful. It was taking longer than usual to fade—she could still hear the bells.

She sat up and almost fell out of bed; it was the telephone, not church bells. She glanced at her bedside clock. It was barely six, and fear raced through her—Dana was in trouble.

She ran into the sitting-room and lifted the receiver. 'What's wrong, Dana?' she asked, feeling as if she had run a mile instead of just a few feet.

'Your perceptions are leading you astray, sister, dear,' Dana mocked. 'Nothing is wrong; on the contrary, everything is very right.'

'I'm glad to hear that,' Claudia said, not believing it for one moment. 'There is something, though—you would hardly ring me up this early just to wish me a happy birthday for tomorrow.' Dana made an exasperated sound and Claudia grinned; it was always she who remembered their joint birthday on time and Dana, who gave elaborate presents, usually a day or so late.

'It's not that early—I've been up for ages, and I'm leaving in a few minutes. I won't be in touch with you for a time and I don't want you starting a panic.'

'Where are you going, Dana?' Claudia said, all her instincts leaping to attention.

'That doesn't concern you and it's best you don't know.' Glaudia groaned; Dana was in one of her teasing moods.

'I don't want to pry into your affairs, but you did ring me and you can't just say you're going away and leave it at that.' Dana chuckled, but Claudia, catching the excitement and apprehension behind the amusement, felt a flicker of unease.

'How does a honeymoon strike you, sister, dear?' Dana purred, and Claudia almost dropped the receiver.

'Are you trying to tell me you're married, Dana? I don't believe you.'

'You'd think you would know,' Dana said sulkily. 'You place far too much importance on this bond that's supposed to exist between twins.'

'You aren't married, are you?' Claudia persisted.

'You don't have to be married to enjoy a honeymoon these days,' Dana jeered. 'Garry and I will get married after his dreary wife gives him a divorce.'

Claudia gripped the phone tightly. Dana was twenty-two and her own mistress, but this sounded serious. Her sister was leaving London with a married man of whom Claudia had never heard.

'Must you run away, Dana—can't you wait until the divorce comes through?'

'That's what you would do, I suppose, but Garry's wife is one of those women who think they have an ideal marriage, and she would go into a decline at the very mention of another woman, so Garry is presenting her with concrete evidence that their marriage is over.'

'That sounds cruel,' Claudia said faintly. 'If the poor woman knows nothing about you it will give her an awful shock.'

'She'll get over it,' Dana said with a callousness that made Claudia shudder. 'Garry has put up with her moaning for years and he's had enough of both her and her brother.'

'Where does the brother come into this?'

'He's Garry's boss and he thinks he can dictate his every move.'

'He could have a point,' Claudia said; Dana only ever saw her own point of view. 'Dana,' Claudia said urgently, 'what about the show at the National Exhibition Centre—you haven't forgotten you're modelling my dress, have you?'

'Trust you to think of your little business above everything else, Claudia! Yes, I had forgotten; you must get someone else, and if you're worrying about my career I'll remind you I'm quite well known in the fashion world and a few weeks' absence won't hurt me in the least.' She banged the receiver down with a force that made Claudia wince.

Claudia put the phone down gently and decided against going back to bed. She would take a bath and go in to work early—there was plenty to do.

The day had seemed longer than usual, Claudia thought as she let herself into her flat with a sigh of relief. She made a cup of tea, and sat down at the table in her tiny kitchen to drink it. She was much too weary to eat or even to open her post; she would do that later.

She spent a pleasant few minutes thinking of her small business where she designed and made exclusive wedding gowns for a rapidly growing circle of customers, but Dana's early-morning phone call refused to be dismissed.

She had felt responsible for her twin since their mother had died two years ago. Fleur Adams had spoilt Dana in every way she could, to the exclusion of Claudia, who had always been closer to her father. She smiled as she remembered the quiet scholar with whom she had shared a love of books. He had died before she'd finished university, but she had carried out the plans they had made. Fleur had encouraged Dana in her ambition to become a model, and she had lived to see her daughter carve a place for herself in the fashion world.

Identical twins were supposed to be very close to each other, and as they were also born under Gemini there was a double bond. Their mother had hated the very thought of anything that could lessen the love between her and Dana, and she had taught her that the bond between them was only imagination on Claudia's part.

Claudia knew it was there and so did Dana, though she wouldn't admit it, and that bond was telling Claudia that Dana was in trouble. Her twin was vulnerable in so many ways that Claudia wasn't. On the surface Dana was hard and self-assured, out for everything she could get, but Claudia knew that exterior wasn't completely genuine. Dana had a soft and clinging side that no one, beside her sister, knew she possessed. At times she didn't seem to know it herself.

This latest escapade could be dangerous for someone like her twin. Dana would be destroyed if anything went wrong with her plan, and to Claudia the whole thing spelt disaster.

The doorbell rang loudly; Claudia put her cup down and got to her feet. That would be her neighbour wanting to chat for a few minutes. She went into the hall, glad of anything that would take her mind from Dana for a few minutes.

She opened the door and stared in astonishment at the tall, strongly built man who was standing with his hand raised for another assault on her bell.

She looked at him in enquiry, rapidly changing to alarm as he asked curtly if she was Miss Adams and, barely waiting for her nod, pushed his way into her small hall, slamming the door behind him.

'What do you think you are doing? I didn't ask you in,' she said, indignation overriding her fear. He stood scowling down at her and Claudia wished she were taller than the five feet eight she had always thought just right.

He was well over six feet, his hair was black and his eyes gleamed amber from between luxuriant lashes. His skin was a golden bronze, as if he spent a lot of time out of doors. His features were strong and rather austere, and his high cheekbones gave him a distinction that was all his own, though the line of his well-cut mouth hinted at a sensuality that disturbed her without her knowing why.

'I don't intend to waste time on useless talk, Miss Adams,' he said harshly. 'I have only one question to ask you and I want a truthful answer.' All Claudia's defences rose to the attack.

'Who do you think you are, bursting into a complete stranger's home and asking questions?' She faltered as she remembered he had called her Miss Adams. 'Who are you?' she demanded. 'You know my name, but I have no idea of yours.'

'You are Miss Claudia Adams, owner of a dress shop and also a model,' he stated, his voice heavy with sarcasm, and Claudia, annoyed that he should call her beautiful showroom a dress shop, didn't bother to tell him she wasn't a model.

'You appear to know who I am, but you still haven't told me who you are or what you want with me.'

'Answer my question, then I will leave you in peace.' He smiled, making her think of a predator waiting to pounce. 'Where is he, Miss Adams?'

Claudia stared at him, wondering if she was dealing with a madman.

'Answer me,' he thundered, and she shivered; her pleasant, familiar room had become a battlefield, and she was on the losing side.

'I don't know what you're talking about,' she said, her tone matching his. 'Who is "he", and why should I know where he is?'

'Don't play games, Miss Adams—you know who I mean well enough, or have you more than one lover you intend running away with?' He came to vibrant life, grasping her arms with such force that she cried out. He shook her sharply, bringing her hard against him.

'Where is Garry. . .where are you meeting him? You must have made plans, so don't try to pretend you're innocent.' His eyes narrowed; Claudia's face mirrored her shock, and he raised a cynical eyebrow.

'You are a good actress, but it won't work with me,' he snarled. He shook her again and she thought she would faint. She cried out and, seeing how white she was, he pushed her on to the settee, following her down and crowding her against the arm. Claudia drew a deep breath and tried to steady her nerves. He was obviously Garry's brother-in-law and he had mistaken her for Dana.

It would be quite simple, she thought frantically, to tell him the truth: that she was not responsible for Dana and she didn't know her plans. Her heart sank as she remembered the phone call which for the first time began to make sense. Dana's voice came back to her with its underlying excitement and what she now realised was fear.

Claudia didn't know Garry, or even his surname; Dana had always had men in her life, but she hadn't seemed serious about any of them, and so far Claudia had hoped in vain that she would find someone to love and to provide the anchor she'd been missing so badly since their mother had died. Now it seemed she had found a man she could love, but he was someone else's husband and her brother was bent on vengeance.

An impatient exclamation brought her aware of the man leaning against the back of the settee in a deceptively relaxed pose. Instinctively she knew that one false move on her part would turn him into a dangerous animal bent on her destruction.

She parted her lips to tell him about Dana, then closed them again as a desperate plea from her twin made itself known as clearly as if Dana had been in the same room. Dana was frightened of this man. Claudia shivered; her twin wasn't alone in her fear, but Dana wouldn't be able to stand up to him for a moment.

Dana had sailed under a blue sky for too long to have any defence against storms, and this man was the worse kind of cyclone. Her lips twitched as she imagined a black cloud, bearing his face, hovering over her head.

'Perhaps you'll share the joke,' he said smoothly, 'and perhaps you will also answer my question? Please don't tell me you've forgotten what it is.'

'I might as well have—I don't know the answer. I take it you are looking for someone?'

'My brother-in-law, as if you didn't know. Now, Miss Adams, cut out the comedy act and tell me where he is.'

'I would, gladly, if I knew; it would appear to be the quickest way of getting rid of you, and that, Mr Whoever-you-are, would give me great pleasure.'

He stretched his long legs out in front of him and looked prepared to stay forever.

'Garry's address or destination, Miss Adams, will remove me immediately.' Claudia sighed.

'I don't know his address or anything about him. You've made a mistake; please go and I'll forget the way you forced your way in here.' She was telling the truth; Dana had given no hint of where they were going. She stole a look at him; he was looking grimmer by the minute—he wouldn't show any mercy once he caught up with the culprits. It would be easy to tell him the truth but that would mean throwing Dana to the wolves, and that she couldn't do.

'How kind,' he said, and Claudia flinched at the sarcasm.

'Look, Mr. . .' Her voice faded away at the sardonic gleam in his eyes.

'Not knowing my name seems to worry you,' he murmured, 'and, while I'm sure you're putting on an act, I'll repeat the information I'm sure you already know. My name is Roman Wyatt, but I won't copy the Americans and say I'm pleased to meet you because I'm not.'

'The feeling is mutual, Mr Wyatt, and the sooner you say goodbye, the sooner we shall both be pleased.' Claudia stood up and made for the door. He was right behind her, as she knew he would be, but she felt more in command on her feet, even though he was far bigger and far more powerful than she was.

'You are a very good actress—I could almost

believe you when you say you don't know Garry,
but the evidence is against you.'

'What evidence, Mr Wyatt? Surely I am to know
of what I am accused, besides wrenching your
brother-in-law from his wife?'

'You cynical little bitch! Doesn't the sanctity of
marriage mean anything to you?' he roared. 'No, of
course it doesn't; I'm a fool to think a woman like
you would give my sister a second thought.'

'You still haven't told me about this evidence you
have against me,' Claudia said with an assumed air
of indifference. She didn't like being thought the
kind of woman who would steal another woman's
husband.

He produced a letter like a conjuror bringing a
rabbit out of a hat, and she didn't know whether she
wanted to laugh or cry. He was really getting to her,
and it wasn't only the accusations he was flinging at
her that were doing the damage. The man himself
was affecting her more powerfully than any other
man had ever done in the whole of her life.

He was magnificent, but she mustn't let the surge
of unexpected excitement running through her blind
her to the danger he could be to Dana. He smoothed
the letter out and held it in front of her.

'I found this on my return from America this
morning; it was followed by a phone call from my
sister—a very emotional phone call, I might add—
and I came here at once.'

The note was a jumble of misspelt and blotched
sentences, and it took her several minutes to
decipher. When she did manage to read it she was
very little wiser. It was full of suspicions, without

one real fact to back them up. She looked up, brows wrinkled in a frown, and he produced a typewritten report and gave it to her. The dates, facts and times, missing from the letter, were all there, and they were damning.

Until now she had clung to the belief that, despite her phone call, Dana was innocent of taking Garry from his wife. The report proved that she had known him very well indeed, and for a very long time.

'Your sister employed a private detective, I suppose?' Claudia said, glancing at the watchful man, who was leaning against the door-frame as if to prevent any thought of escape she might have.

'No, I did, and the evidence is very clear. It proves you spent at least three weekends together as man and wife in the Cotswolds. I'm surprised you didn't come here, but I expect you wanted to keep a façade of respectability. It was some time before the detective found your address; you've been very clever in not meeting here, but it was careless of you to go to the same hotel every time, even if you did sign in as Mr and Mrs Smith. Smith. . .couldn't either of you think of anything better than that?'

'Obviously not, but I am not and never have been Mrs Smith, and there is nothing to prove differently.'

'Mrs Smith is a model and she also runs a shop in Solihull; coincidence doesn't go that far, Miss Adams.'

'I can only assure you that you have the wrong person, Mr Wyatt; there are many models, and more than a few work in the Midlands, and several must have other business interests. Now please go.' He

passed a hand over his face, his expression hard, but
she could detect a deep weariness in his fine eyes:

'I will do as you ask for now—jet lag is catching
up with me—but I warn you not to try to disappear;
your every move will be known to me almost before
you make it.'

He left so quickly that she stared in astonishment
at the door he had closed behind him. She could
hardly believe he had gone—he had seemed set for
the night—and, to her consternation, the flat
seemed empty and cold without his disturbing but
magnetic presence.

A yawn took her by surprise; her long day and the
worry about Dana, to say nothing of the arrival of
Roman Wyatt, had finally caught up with her. She
went to bed and surprisingly, for she had thought
her worry over Dana would keep her awake, she
slept at once, to awaken with Dana's voice echoing
in her head. She switched on the bedside lamp and
looked dazedly at the clock. Two o'clock. She
groaned and turned over, hoping she would fall
asleep again, but her brain insisted on relaying
pictures of her twin, so vividly that Dana could have
been in the same room.

Since their mother's death Claudia had hoped to
come closer to her sister, but Dana had the world at
her feet and she laughed at all Claudia's attempts to
resurrect the bond they had shared as children.
However, to Claudia, Dana was part of her—
together they formed a whole that few sisters could
hope to achieve.

The drift apart had been gradual. Their mother
had been a fashion model before her marriage; she

had always regretted giving it up, and she had seen, in her daughters, the means of reliving her career, this time successfully.

Dana had embraced the dancing and singing lessons with fervour, but Claudia, trailing behind her sister, had been bored to tears by them, and after a time her father had put an end to what he'd seen as a waste of his money and Claudia's time.

From then on the twins took different paths. Claudia, with her love of beauty and skill at drawing, was swept into her father's world of libraries and museums, and, while Dana took lessons in make-up and posture Claudia enrolled in art school.

I should have made more effort to get close to her, Claudia thought miserably; all her efforts had been rebuffed, but, deny it or not, the bond was there and she hesitated to turn her sensitive twin over to Roman Wyatt's not so tender mercy.

Roman Wyatt. . .there was a man who could model for the hero of any romantic novel, if, that was, you liked all that raw sexual power. Claudia didn't; her idea of a man was someone gentle and loving. She shook her head sharply—Dana had once accused her of being afraid of men.

'You are so closed into your fairy-tale world of happy ever after that you'll never bring yourself to form a relationship with a flesh and blood man; you're half dead, Claudia; you live surrounded by wedding dresses, but you'll never be able to bring yourself to wear one. Grow up, sister, and come into the real world.' Her mocking laughter sounded as clear now as it had done months earlier.

Dana could be right—she did find it difficult to

get friendly with any of the men she had met so far, but that didn't mean she never would. She sighed, closed her eyes, and drifted to sleep.

The morning looked bright with the promise of a sunny day to come. Claudia dressed in a dark green cotton dress clasped round her slender waist with a broad yellow belt, drank a cup of coffee and opened her neglected post.

It contained several birthday cards, but Dana's was late, as usual. She laughed at the one from Myra; it depicted the Gemini star sign—twins, one laughing, one thoughtful. Claudia sighed; Geminis were dual characters, and being twins made it even worse.

She walked to work, hoping that the troubles of the day before had vanished with the night. She resolved to ring Dana as soon as she got to the showroom. Dana would laugh and say she had been teasing, and they would talk about the big show for charity where Dana would model the wedding gown Claudia had designed.

The show was called 'Designed To Help' and it was to be held at the NEC. Top designers from all over the country were getting together to stage something that, it was already forecast, would be the money-raising event of the year. Dana wouldn't give up the chance to shine in front of all the heads of the fashion world.

She wouldn't tell Dana about Roman Wyatt; there would be no need to bring that horrible man into their conversartion. She faltered as she remembered the dreadful report he had shown her. She flung her head back and resumed her graceful stride. The

detective must be mistaken. Garry had left home
with someone, but not with Dana.

She paused just inside her showroom, looking
round with a sense of achievement. It had been
barely two years since she had opened it with the
money her father had left her. She had always loved
to sew, and when she had started to design in earnest
wedding dresses had proved irresistible. Her mother
had thought she would fail and had pinned all her
hopes on Dana, who'd begun to attract the attention
of the Press.

'Good morning—happy birthday!' Myra
Stephens, Claudia's chief assistant, bustled in, her
round smiling face and dancing dark curls making
Claudia smile too, her spirits lifting at once. She
returned Myra's greeting, thanking her for the card.

Myra gave her a gaily wrapped parcel, and
Claudia opened it to find a beautiful silk scarf
printed with white and pink roses on a jade-green
background.

'It's lovely, Myra; thank you very much,' Claudia
said, hardly able to speak. Her twin, the person
closest to her, hadn't even sent her a card, while
Myra had chosen this perfect gift.

'I love roses,' she said, hoping Myra hadn't
noticed how much her thoughtful gesture had
affected her.

'Roses are one of the Gemini flowers,' Myra said
happily. 'I'm glad you like the scarf.'

'I do, very much; thank you again.' Claudia put
the scarf carefully to one side and launched into the
first task of the day, the ordering of silks and lace
from London, Italy and France.

Within an hour the two women had decided which patterns to order, and Myra settled at her typewriter while Claudia perched on the edge of her desk to phone Dana. The telephone rang on and on. Claudia frowned, an icy feeling of trouble to come stealing over her. She replaced the phone on its rest and looked up to see Myra gazing at her, a concerned look on her face.

'Is anything the matter, Claudia?' she asked quietly, and Claudia found herself telling her about Dana's early-morning phone call. She didn't mention Roman Wyatt—she couldn't talk about him without wanting to scream.

'It's time Dana took responsibility for her own life, instead of turning to you at every imagined crisis,' Myra said. Claudia looked at her in surprise; this was the first time Myra had ventured to criticise Dana, and she wasn't sure she liked it.

'I know I shouldn't say anything, but I've known you both for a long time, and your mother spoiled Dana rotten. What if she has run off with this Garry? She's not a child.'

'Garry's married, and his brother-in-law thinks I know where he is,' Claudia said, breaking her determination not to mention Roman Wyatt.

'You're not Dana's keeper. It's not my business, but I strongly advise you to have nothing to do with the whole thing; divorce can be very messy.' Myra paused, struck by Claudia's stillness.

'You're already involved, aren't you? Is there anything I can do to help?' Claudia shook her head, grateful for the other woman's offer. If only Dana had been more like Myra. She shook off the treacherous thought; Dana was her twin and she loved her with all her faults—goodness knew, she had enough of her own.

'Mr Wyatt has mistaken me for Dana,' she said simply.

'But surely you told him you were her sister? No, I can see by your expression that you didn't. There's more to this than a missing husband, isn't there?'

'There must be, but I don't know what it is. Mr Wyatt is determined to find his brother-in-law and I don't want that to happen when Dana is with him.'

'I understand how you feel, but I think it would do your sister the world of good to come face to face with reality for once.'

Secretly Claudia had a sneaky feeling that Myra could be right, but she wasn't going to tell her so. Myra inserted a fresh sheet of paper into her typewriter.

'What are you going to do?'

'Other than allow Roman Wyatt to think I'm Dana? I don't know; I can only hope that, by the time he realises I'm not her, the whole thing will have blown over.'

'Wouldn't it be best to tell him the truth? It won't lead him to Dana, and it will save your tender conscience.'

Claudia laughed. 'You know me too well, Myra, and you could be right. I just hope it's resolved before the show—if Dana doesn't surface we shall be short of our top model.' She rubbed a hand over her eyes. 'Phone the agencies, will you, and see if they can come up with someone, just in case?'

'I'll try, but I don't think I'll have much luck—the best models will have been booked for months.'

'Just try. I haven't given up on Dana yet.'

'From what you've told me, I don't think we'll see her for a long time unless your Mr Wyatt finds them, and while he thinks you are Dana he won't be looking very hard, will he?'

Claudia shrugged her shoulders. 'I know, but what else can I do? Dana couldn't stand up to him for a moment.'

'You can, I suppose?' Myra said drily. 'Take care, Claudia; you're more vulnerable than you think you are, and he sounds a very determined man.' Myra was right, Claudia thought as she attended to a customer. Where Roman Wyatt was concerned she was like a snail without a shell. She had never been so aware of anyone as she was of the powerful man who had entered her life so abruptly. She could only hope that when he had recovered from jet lag he would have second thoughts and leave Garry to go his own way.

She recalled his expression as he had accused her of knowing where Garry was, and she knew he wasn't the kind of man to give up easily. Fortunately the rest of the day was so busy that she was able to push Dana and her problems to the back of her mind.

Roman Wyatt wasn't so easily dismissed; his strong dark face and amber eyes danced between her and the dress she was designing and materialised when she was talking to customers, but despite everything it was a satisfying day business-wise, and she said goodnight to Myra with a feeling of achievement.

It was time she also called it a day; she would continue with the work she was doing after she'd eaten. She picked up her bag, switched off the lights and locked the door behind her. She dropped the keys into her bag and straightened up, a small cry escaping her as she walked straight into a large solid body. She opened her mouth to scream, only to let her breath out with a hiss.

'Oh, it's you, Mr Wyatt,' she said in disgust. 'What do you mean by frightening the life out of me?'

'People in your position lay themselves open to fear,' he said softly, and Claudia's nerves started to tingle once more.

'What do you want? I've had a busy day and I want my dinner. I've no wish to stand here talking in riddles.' She glared at him; he was even larger than she remembered. Last night he had been suffering from jet lag; now he seemed to be fully recovered, and power flowed from him in waves.

'I'll take you home—we need to talk.' He put a hand under her arm and turned her towards a silver-grey Rolls that took up all the parking space outside her shop.

'I'll walk, thank you,' she snapped. 'We said far too much yesterday and I see no reason for more of the same. You have the wrong person, Mr Wyatt. I'm a hard-working dress designer, not a scarlet woman.'

'No? I think you're the woman I'm looking for,

and I'm not going away until you give me what I
want. Now do you come quietly or do I use force?'

'In broad daylight? Don't push your luck,' she
said, her words ending in a wail as he picked her up
and dumped her in the car like an unwieldly parcel.
He moved so rapidly that by the time she had
recovered enough to scream they were driving
towards her flat.

'You won't get away with treating me like this,'
she said, grinding her teeth together with fury.

'No? Who's going to stop me?'

'I have neighbours,' Claudia said, remembering
with dismay that the young couple on the top floor
were away and Mrs Gregson was staying with her
sister overnight.

'I've done my homework,' he remarked, and her
heart sank into her smart sandals as she realised that
he was aware her neighbours were away.

CHAPTER TWO

AT THAT point Claudia gave up trying to fight Roman—physically, at least. She would tell him he had mistaken her for Dana and then he would leave. She sat up straight as they reached her flat, prepared to act with dignity. He couldn't eat her, and she didn't think he would murder her either.

An hour later she wasn't so sure about the latter. He had settled down on the settee, watching her every move as she'd put the kettle on and taken salad and cold meat from the fridge. She laid two places, looking at him enquiringly, and he nodded, his eyes narrowing.

'If you're asking me to share your meal, I accept; we can postpone our discussion until afterwards.'

'I'm not doing you a favour,' Claudia snapped. 'I'm too hungry to wait until you leave, and by the same token I'm going to change. You can make the tea when the kettle boils.' He raised an eyebrow and looked her over from head to toe.

'Wear that green silky thing you had on last night,' he drawled. 'Your morals might reek of the dustbin, but the scenery is magnificent.'

Claudia bit back the words she dearly wanted to use, contenting herself by banging and locking the bathroom door. Needless to say, she put on jeans and a loose jade top, not the revealing gown he had requested she wear.

He raised a sardonic eyebrow as she sat down opposite him and started to eat. Hungry as she was, Claudia found it difficult to do justice to the meal. She was far too conscious of the man whose own appetite seemed unimpaired by any of the emotions that were troubling her more and more.

At last unable to bear the closeness the small table forced on them, she took her plate through to the kitchen, returning with a tray of coffee. She poured out and, placing one cup in front of him, took hers into the sitting-room.

She made for an armchair, knowing it would be wise to keep him at a distance, but she didn't reach it. An arm, clad in a golden-brown shirt that she had already noticed did marvellous things for his dark hair and amber eyes, transferred her smoothly to the settee, without her spilling a drop of coffee.

He followed her down, trapping her against the upholstered arm and his hard muscular body. She felt rage flood through her and she fought down the impulse to scream—that was just what he was waiting for. Instead she sipped her coffee slowly, a small smile on her lips as she saw his expectation of the scene he was sure she would make slowly die.

'You wanted to talk about something, I believe,' she said, her voice as smooth as cream, and something leapt to life in his eyes at the confidence she was showing.

'You still maintain you are not the woman with whom Garry is having an affair?' he asked, and she shivered at the threat in his quiet voice.

'I do; I don't even know him.'

'Then how do you explain this?' he said, reaching

for a folder that she hadn't noticed lying at the end
of the settee. He took out a large photograph and
placed it on her knee, taking her cup from her with
the same effortless movement.

Claudia stared at what looked like a photograph
of herself in a revealing and over-elaborate evening
dress. It wasn't her, it was Dana, but a photograph
always emphasised their likeness to each other.
Claudia could never believe she was as lovely as the
girl in the picture whose cloud of shining golden-
brown hair flowed over the translucent skin of her
shoulders like a caress. Blue eyes smiled from a face
that, while not strictly beautiful, was vital and alive.
Her mouth hinted at a passion Claudia had never
known, and the curve of her breasts above the green
silk promised the fulfilment of every man's dream.
Claudia didn't care to dress in such revealing clothes,
but Dana was a model and her looks were her chief
asset.

He took the photograph from her, replacing it
with another one. Claudia gasped; it was Dana
again, but this time she wasn't alone. Her black satin
dress left nothing to the imagination, and neither did
the way the man with her was gazing into her eyes.

They had obviously just finished dancing, and just
as obviously their next stop would be the nearest
double bed. Claudia raised her eyes to the man
whose own eyes were fixed with deadly intent on
her, and silently asked Dana's forgiveness for what
she was about to do.

'I was half inclined to believe you last night until I
received these this morning,' he said, and the hidden
violence in his voice made her go cold. 'You must

put it down to jet lag and worry over my sister; I'm
not usually so easily fooled.'

'That isn't me—it's my twin sister,' Claudia said
simply, to be immediately disconcerted by the dis-
believing look in his eyes.

'You don't believe me, do you? I assure you it's
true. Dana is the model; I only make dresses.' She
touched Dana's pictured face gently with the tip of
one slender finger.

'You're right, I don't believe you, not now, not
ever.' Claudia shrugged; it was what she had
expected. The evidence was too damning for anyone
who didn't know of Dana's existence, but she
couldn't help feeling briefly disappointed. Beyond
all reason, she had wanted him to believe her.

'That's Garry, I take it.' Her finger jabbed at the
picture of the man, not quite touching it, and he
picked up the difference in the gestures immediately.

'Can't you even stroke his picture for fear I shall
see how much you miss him, or is all your love kept
for yourself?' He pulled her hard against him, and
for a moment passion gleamed from brilliant golden
eyes before they went cold and blank and he pushed
her violently from him.

'I must be going mad,' he muttered. 'For a
moment I disbelieved the evidence of my own eyes.'
Claudia wished she could stop shaking; the touch of
his hard body against hers had started up a whirlpool
of emotion that left her wanting to run until she had
put miles between them.

'I will ask you once more for my brother-in-law's
address,' he said, his voice as cold as the Arctic
snows. She stole a glance at him; his features

matched the ice in his tone and his eyes surpassed it. She faced him calmly, her head high, though she couldn't meet his eyes.

'I can only repeat that you're wasting your time with me. I'm not the woman in the picture; she is my sister Dana.'

'That's rubbish—even identical twins aren't such perfect images of each other.'

'Dana and I have always been photocopies,' Claudia said wearily. 'She doesn't like it, but the fact remains.' Roman looked uncertain, his superb self-confidence shaken. He recovered quickly and shook his head.

'I don't believe you for a moment; even if I did, you're my only lead and I'm not going to let you out of my sight until I catch up with Garry. You're the bait for the jackal, and sooner or later he'll come for you, and when he does I intend to be there.'

He walked over to the mantelpiece and stood looking at her cards, a cynical smile twisting his lips.

'You come under the sign for twins, if this card is anything to go by,' he said, picking up the card Myra had sent. 'I give you full marks for a vivid imagination but. . .' He paused and flicked the card to her. 'If you really do have a twin then the chances of finding Garry can only be better if you're with me.' The gauntlet had been flung in clear sight of them both, and where they went from there Claudia hadn't the faintest idea.

'Stalemate is the word I think you want,' she said, congratulating herself on her dry tone. He laughed, a sound devoid of amusement.

'Quite right, my dear Claudia.' She jumped at

hearing her name on his lips. He read her expression correctly and laughed again.

'We're going to be close to each other for the next few days, perhaps longer, and I refuse to keep calling you Miss Adams; Claudia is a charming name.'

'My father was a professor of Roman studies and he chose it,' she said automatically, but then her eyes flicked to his in alarm. 'What do you mean by saying we're going to be close to each other? You're the last person I want to be near, Mr Wyatt.'

'That's too bad, Claudia, because I'm going to be your second skin until you lead me to Garry.' Claudia looked at him in horror.

'I'll spell it out for you,' he said as gently as one would to a young child. 'We are staying together until either Garry or this mythical twin of yours contacts you.'

'No way; I won't let you stay here,' Claudia said, pulling out of the paralysis that gripped her. 'My neighbours on the top floor return tomorrow, and Mrs Gregson is here now—one good scream and she'll send for the police.'

'Thank you for warning me; it's time I put plan B into action.' And before she could utter so much as a squeak he clapped his hand over her mouth, swung her into his arms, and they were out of the flat and into his car without so much as a curtain twitching. Claudia pressed the door-handle in vain as Roman laughed at her efforts.

'The door operates from a central switch, and it's locked.'

'Where are you taking me?' she said, anger making her eyes flash.

'Somewhere we won't be disturbed while we finish our talk.' He sounded and looked implacable. Claudia stared at her linked fingers and planned to get away as soon as they stopped. She didn't like the sound of the 'second skin' bit at all, and the way he had kidnapped her had been terrifying. He would have to stop some time, and then she would be able to escape.

Her plan was doomed to failure; they drove to the outskirts of Solihull and turned into the underground garage belonging to a newly built block of flats that were the last word in luxury, according to the advertisement she had seen.

He had the passenger door open before she could free herself from the seatbelt. He scooped her up, and she was in a lift, jammed tightly against him, before she could catch her breath. They travelled speedily to the top floor and she watched the numbers changing with a feeling of despair.

'This lift only goes to the penthouse,' he mocked as they came to a smooth halt. 'The friend who's lent me his flat likes his privacy.' He certainly did; the lift opened into a square red-carpeted hall and she couldn't even hear anyone else. The sitting-room was long, and looked as if a child had been let loose with buckets of primary colours. It made Claudia stare for a moment, but she was too concerned with the man who had forced her here to worry about other people's bad taste.

'This has gone too far,' she stormed, rounding on him like a vengeful fury. 'How dare you kidnap me?'

'I dare anything to help Berenice,' he said, not in the least disturbed by her rage.

'Your wife won't like you acting as my second skin.'

His eyes crinkled with amusement. 'I'm not married—my sister Berenice is my only relative, but I'm intrigued by your interest, though you could have just asked me instead of getting angry.'

'I'm not interested,' she said, knowing she wasn't telling the whole truth. She had wanted to know if he had a wife, just out of normal curiosity, ever since she had first met him. He was watching her intently, standing with one hand on the back of a chair, looking perfectly relaxed, but it was the deceptive ease of a panther and could change in a flash.

'You have achieved your objective, Mr Wyatt, so can we have this talk you insist upon and go our separate ways?'

'You haven't been listening, Claudia; we're not parting for one moment until I find Garry—and it's time you called me Roman.'

'I prefer "Mr Wyatt"; I only call friends by their first names.'

'And lovers,' he said softly. 'Before you say we're not lovers, Claudia, remember that many things are possible in this world, though it will take a miracle to make me forget whose lover you really are.'

'Your brother-in-law and I are——' Claudia started to say, biting her words off short. He didn't believe she had a sister, and if he thought she was involved with Garry it would be a barrier he would hesitate to breach. 'I trust you will remember to think along those lines,' she said instead, and his eyes flashed at her tone.

'My brother-in-law's name is Garry Turner—you seem to have difficulty in remembering it,' he said cynically, waving her to a chair. After a moment's hesitation she sat in one of the large armchairs, half expecting to be pushed on to the settee, but he allowed her to sit alone, only raising an eyebrow as he lowered himself into the matching chair.

The doorbell rang, making her jump up—this could be her chance, but Roman reached the door first. She stared in astonishment as a waiter pushed a drinks trolley into the room. Roman pulled her close to his side as he thanked the man, tipping him lavishly.

Claudia stood silent as the waiter left. Roman's fingers biting into her waist told her he wasn't going to allow her any opportunity to talk. His eyes were on her mouth, promising retribution in the form of a punishing kiss if she attempted to speak.

'We'll eat before we talk. I'm sure you're as ready for a drink as I am.' Claudia would have liked to refuse but she needed to steady her nerves.

'Now we'll talk,' Roman said later as they settled back in the chairs. He crossed one long leg over the other, and she was conscious of how virile and masculine he was.

'As you have gathered, I plan to be with you every waking and sleeping moment—oh, you don't need to worry, I have no designs on your body, delectable though it is. I just intend to know your every move.' Claudia sighed as he continued to speak.

'I don't want to spend my time with you, any more

than you want me at your side, so the sooner you tell me where Garry is, the sooner we can part company. Even a woman like you won't want to be responsible for what could happen to my sister if I don't find him soon.' He leaned forward, and Claudia was struck by the sincerity behind his worrying statement.

'I don't know what you mean by "a woman like you",' she said, more gently than she had intended. 'Any more than I understand why it's so important for you to find Garry. He isn't the first man to leave his wife and, though I understand your instinct to protect your sister, surely she could and should fight her own battles?'

Roman looked as if he was about to pounce; she cringed back in her chair, and he frowned.

'Don't look so scared; I'm not going to beat you— yet,' he said softly. 'Though I'm tempted when you persist in playing the innocent.'

'I'm not playing games, Mr Wyatt; I know nothing about your sister and I certainly don't wish her any harm.' He looked at her with hard eyes that seemed to see every thought she had ever had. After a few moments she could stand it no longer, and with an effort she wrenched her gaze away and looked down at the carpet.

'Very well, Miss Adams, I'll give you the benefit of the doubt and concede that you don't know why my sister needs her husband's support so badly.' He looked intently into her eyes. 'If she doesn't get it she will almost certainly lose the child she is carrying.'

Claudia cried out, and his eyes widened at the shock mirrored on her face.

'Perhaps I have misjudged you. Is it possible you don't know that Berenice has had three miscarriages and that with every one her chance of carrying a child to term diminishes?'

'I swear to you that I didn't know anything about it. . .neither can my sister know, or she wouldn't have gone with Garry.'

'I almost begin to believe you didn't know about Berenice, but I still don't believe in a sister who doesn't exist,' he said slowly. 'Berenice is obsessional about having a child, and Garry has grown increasingly impatient. I can see his point in a way; he likes a full social life. . .and he doesn't want to sit at home with a wife who is depressed and can only talk about babies.' Claudia knew, instinctively, that if Roman were in Garry's place his reactions would be very, very different. She didn't know if he wanted a wife and children, but she knew that, having set his hand to any task, he would carry it through to the end. She laughed silently at herself; she had only known him for a few hours, and here she was, assessing his character as if he were an old and true friend.

'My sister thinks Garry is abroad,' he said, answering the question she hadn't liked to ask. 'I've told her he's travelling between America and Mexico and can't be reached for a few days. I've also assured her that his involvement with another woman was only a temporary madness. Berenice has high blood-pressure; she has to remain in hospital because of stress, or she will miscarry, and if that happens I fear for her mental health.' He leaned forward and took her hands in his.

'Now will you tell me where Garry is?'

'I can't,' Claudia said, watching his expression grow dark.

'I only wish I could. Please, you must believe I don't even *know* Garry Turner.'

'You are a hard-hearted liar,' he rapped. 'You look like an angel but you're helping to destroy another woman without turning a hair. Garry must be a much better lover than I would have thought him, or is it the legacy his godfather has left him that tempts you?'

He threw her hand contemptuously from him and she rubbed it, wondering if she would ever get rid of the impression of his fingers. She couldn't bear him to think she was so selfish that she didn't care what harm she caused. She reminded herself that the guilt, if there was any, belonged to Dana, but she couldn't believe her twin knew about Berenice.

'Dana can't know about your sister; if she did she would insist Garry return to his wife,' she said as sincerely as she could. To her consternation, he laughed, and ice washed over her at the harsh sound.

'Nice try, Claudia, but not good enough. Two women looking like you would be impossible.' He got up and poured more drinks from the trolley in a corner of the room, placing one in front of her.

'Drink, Claudia—I'm sure you need it after your flight of fancy.'

Claudia stared at him helplessly. 'I'm telling you the truth,' she said gently. 'Your detective has made a mistake.'

'In that case, you'll be able to tell me where this

look-alike woman is. No?' as she shook her head. 'I
thought not.'

The mockery made her wish she'd said nothing—
she hadn't helped Berenice, Dana or herself. He
was far more suspicious of her now than he had been
before she'd told him about Dana, and he still
thought she was Garry's lover.

'I give you full marks for trying—your imagination
does you credit—but you forget I've had both you
and Garry watched; if there were two of you I would
know.'

That was puzzling Claudia, but a moment's reflection gave her the answer. The detective wouldn't be
expecting two of them and, when Dana had been
appearing as a model in London, Claudia would
have been in Solihull. It would be natural to take it
for granted that the model and the dress designer
were one and the same.

'I can't make you believe in Dana, but neither of
us would hurt your sister,' Claudia said. All at once
she wasn't so sure of her twin's reaction. Dana had
always had a fine sense of her own importance, and
Claudia wasn't certain she would consider another
woman's need before her own desires. She pushed
the thought violently from her. Dana wasn't like
that. She got to her feet.

'It's time I went home, Mr Wyatt. I have a
business to run and a home of my own, which I
prefer to this rather flashy place of yours.'

He grimaced and raised his hands in self-defence,
a little of his dark mood dropping away, giving her a
glimpse of the man he could be if he weren't so
concerned for his sister.

'This isn't mine. Denzil always did like bright colours. I assure you, I don't go for scarlet chairs, black carpets and purple and pink curtains, any more than you do.'

'That's beside the point. I want to go home.'

'Sorry Claudia, I can't risk it; if we stayed at your flat you would try to bring your neighbours to your rescue. No, we stay here.'

'I don't want to stay anywhere with you. If I promise to let you know if your brother-in-law contacts me surely you'll call off this business of staying together like two ill-matched peas in one small pod?'

'I'm not so sure we're ill-matched, and I don't think you are either,' he said with a brooding look that made her shudder.

'You don't like me. I'm the woman you still think is involved with your sister's husband, remember?' she said hastily as his fingers closed round her wrist.

'Thank you for reminding me,' he said, dropping her hand as if he had grasped something distasteful. 'I don't know why I keep forgetting who and what you are, but I promise you, my memory will improve from now on.' He turned to a door at the end of the room.

'I'll show you where you can sleep. Don't make any fuss—I'm not in the mood.' Claudia took one look at him and decided to do as she was told, for the moment. The décor of the room he showed her into was a complete contrast to that of the sitting-room, but just as garish.

'Would you like a drink before you go to bed?' he asked politely, and she found she was nodding. She couldn't think why—the last thing she wanted was to prolong her time in his company. The sight of the handbag she'd caught up as he'd carried her from her flat and which he had tossed on to the bed gave her the glimmering of an idea. She picked it up and turned casually to the dressing-table. Myra always said Geminis were good with ideas, and if this one worked it could solve her immediate problems.

'I'd like a cup of coffee, if it's not too much trouble. Perhaps you'll join me?' She held her breath while he considered the suggestion, relaxing when he smiled.

'Why not? Come through when you're ready.' Claudia expelled a pent-up breath as he disappeared. She looked in the mirror, exclaiming in dismay at her appearance. Her hair was falling round her shoulders and her eyes were bright with apprehension. She only needed an evening gown like the one Dana wore in the magazine picture and no one would belive there were two of them. Not that Roman did anyway, she reflected gloomily.

She hurriedly tidied her hair, pulling it back until it hurt and securing the tight knot with pins. For the first time she regretted being an identical twin; none of this would have happened if she and Dana had been ordinary sisters, but then you might never have met Roman Wyatt, her subconscious whispered. That would be a very good thing, she shouted back, but her inner self didn't agree and, muttering under her breath at her unruly self, she pushed unanswerable questions to the back of her mind and got down to business.

She emptied the contents of her bag on to the

bed, smiling ruefully at the conglomeration of articles, some of which she had carried about forever. That diary, for instance, seven months out of date, the lipstick she no longer wore, several letters waiting to be answered and a charity appeal leaflet. . .and, ah, yes, there it was.

Her fingers closed round the small bottle of sleeping tablets Dana had been prescribed when she had stayed with Claudia after a bout of flu. Claudia had taken them from her when she'd discovered her sister was making no effort to sleep naturally. They would come in very useful now.

She slipped two of the tablets into the pocket of her jeans and, leaving her bag on the bed, sauntered into the kitchen.

'I thought you'd forgotten your coffee and had decided to go to bed instead,' he said, looking disapprovingly at her freshly done hair. 'That's not an improvement—I prefer your hair as it is in your photograph.' He put two earthenware mugs on the table and calmly took the pins from her hair. He ran his fingers through her curls and stepped back to admire his handiwork.

'That's better. I want you to wear it like that always.' Claudia battled with the urge to crown him with the coffee, only restraining herself by thinking of her plans.

'You've got a nerve,' she snapped. 'I shall wear my hair how I please.'

'Not while you live with me,' he said quietly, and she couldn't decide if he was serious or not. She glared at him, but there was too much at stake to risk a fight, so after a moment she pushed her hair away from her face and sat down, pulling one of the mugs towards her.

'Very wise,' he said maddeningly. 'I hope your coffee is to your liking?' Claudia stirred and sipped before replying.

'As a matter of fact, it's not. I'd like some more milk, please.' He got up, casting her a smile that said women were never pleased, and moved over to the fridge, his back to her.

Claudia dived into her pocket, dropped the sleeping pills into the mug, stirred swiftly and rapidly switched the mugs round.

She was stirring the coffee in front of her, an innocent expression on her face as he came back to the table. Roman put the milk jug in front of her, his fingers slipped and the milk spilt all over the table. He looked at the spreading white pool helplessly, and Claudia leapt to her feet to avoid the liquid splashing her jeans.

'I'll get a cloth,' she said as he made no effort to deal with the mess.

'There's a towel in the drawer by the sink.' He came to life and made a half-hearted attempt to mop the milk up with his handkerchief. Claudia raced for the towel; he was still standing in the same place and still looking helpless as she dealt briskly with the spill.

'Is there enough milk left for you?' he said as she sat down once more.

'Plenty,' she said, adding some to her mug. She lifted it to her lips and swallowed. 'You should drink yours—it's not very hot,' she said, trying hard not to show how anxious she was. She must have been

successful, she crowed to herself as he tossed his
drink down quickly. She finished her own coffee,
listening to him as he began to talk about his friend
Denzil. She lost the thread of the conversation after
a time.

Her mind was too concerned with the man who
was tilting his chair back as he talked, one slim
bronzed hand emphasising a point now and again.
He was a compelling man, overwhelmingly masculine, and in any other circumstances she would have
been attracted—no, more than just attracted to him.
As it was, he represented danger, both to herself
and to Dana.

She was also in danger of falling asleep. She
snapped to attention and glared at Roman—he was
the one who was going to sleep; she must remain
alert. She pushed her mug away from her and said
she was going to bed. She yawned, to show how
tired she was, and to her dismay found her excuse
was genuine. She was so weary that it was all she
could do not to put her head down on the table and
close her eyes.

She walked towards the door with an effort,
glancing at Roman for signs that he too was on the
verge of sleep. He was watching her, an enigmatic
expression on his face that made her wary, even
though it was hard to keep her eyes open. This was
all wrong. . .she shouldn't be the one to feel drowsy.

'You. . .you. . .' she managed before, to her
horror, she felt herself falling. She was caught and
held in a firm warm grasp and she turned her face
into a broad comforting shoulder as the blackness
descended.

CHAPTER THREE

CLAUDIA woke up slowly, opening her eyes and closing them immediately against the light that poured in through long narrow windows. Her head felt muzzy; her tongue had been used as a mop for an unspeakable floor; a headache was hovering, waiting to pounce; this room wasn't hers and neither was the shirt she was wearing.

She shot upright, clutching her head as it throbbed in protest at her sudden move. Her gaze went, unbelievingly, from the pink and blue polka-dot material draping the dressing-table to the bright pink carpet patterned with impossible blue roses and on to the royal-blue wallpaper with its equally impossible pink pansies.

'If you think this is awful you should see the master suite,' a cheerful voice said, and she lifted her head to see a fit-looking Roman lounging at the end of her bed.

'You drugged me,' she accused, and he grinned.

'So I did, with the coffee you had laced with sleeping pills for me. Don't you know it's dangerous to do that? I could have been allergic or something.'

'So could I.'

'Hardly likely—they were your pills.'

'No, they aren't, they belong to Dana.'

'This other woman who isn't you and who has run away with Garry in your place. I don't believe it;

43

identical twins aren't such perfect copies of each other.' Claudia groaned and held her head, which was holding a big-band concert of its own.

Impossible as it seemed, he still thought she was lying, or was he pretending in order to keep her with him? Unbidden excitement flowered deep inside her, only to die. He was attracted to her but a man like Roman Wyatt didn't need to play tricks to keep a woman near him.

'Headache?' he said without a trace of sympathy. 'You brought it on yourself. . .however, I'm not inhuman, even where you are concerned. Get dressed. I'll have something ready that should make you feel better, and, before you ask me, yes, I did undress you and put you into my shirt. You have a beautiful body, one I'd enjoy getting to know thoroughly in other circumstances,' he said as he closed the door quietly behind him.

Claudia gritted her teeth together, groaning as she blushed from head to foot. The bastard hadn't left her an ounce of pride. It should have been him nursing a headache, not her. It didn't take the Brain of Britain to deduce that he had known, somehow, that she had drugged his coffee, and full marks to his rapier mind—he had turned the tables, or rather the mugs, very neatly.

She walked into the kitchen feeling like committing murder, Roman Wyatt's murder. He hadn't quite stripped her, but the lacy bra and briefs he had left her with could have proved no barrier to his imagination.

She sat down at the table and looked with disfavour at the glass in front of her. Under his gaze, which dared her to object, she drank it reluctantly. Minutes after, she thought she might just live. She nibbled the toast he gave her unenthusiastically, but she had to admit it helped—her head was now using muffled drums.

'How did you know about the coffee?' she asked, keeping her eyes on her plate.

'How could I not? You advertised your every move.I knew you'd thought of something, and when you asked for extra milk it wasn't hard to guess what it was.'

Devious devil; she should have known better than to think she could fool him. A clock struck and she counted the chimes. Eleven; that couldn't be right.

'It can't be that time,' she said, bounding up, only to clutch at the table as her head started up again.

'It is, but don't worry, I've phoned your assistant. She's very sorry you aren't well, but not surprised; apparently she's been urging you to take a holiday for the last two years.'

Claudia looked at him sourly. 'You had no right to say anything to Myra, let alone encourage her to give you my life story.'

'She didn't do that, but I'm sure that with a bit more time she would have. I expect you want to go to work?' he said abruptly.

'I do, and I suppose you're going to stop me?'

'On the contrary, I'll take you there. I also have a business to run.'

Claudia straightened her spine carefully; that was the best bit of news since she had met the overpowering Roman Wyatt. 'You've decided to finish this ridiculous business of keeping tabs on me, then?'

'Not at all; you haven't given me what I want, and until you do I am your other self.'

'You said I could go to work,' Claudia accused.

'So you can. I'll pick you up at five—that will give you time to arrange the holiday the delightful Myra thinks you should have.'

'I can't take a holiday in June—you must be out of your mind! It's one of our busiest times, and there's this NEC show in three weeks.'

'Your Myra sounds very capable; she said you were ahead with your designing and you have a good stock. She also said she could deal with any fresh orders.' Claudia scowled; he *had* been busy.

'Is there anything about me or my business you don't know?' she said bitterly.

'I suspect a good deal, but by the time I've tracked Garry down you'll be an open book. Don't get me wrong, I shall be only too pleased to be able to slam you shut and return you to the darkest corner of my mind.'

There seemed to be nothing to say to that. He sounded as if he was thoroughly disgusted by the whole business and she felt a pang of dismay. People usually liked her, but Roman Wyatt regarded her with loathing and she knew that wasn't how she wanted him to think of her.

'What about your business. . .won't it suffer if you take a holiday?'

'I have good managers,' he said, the corners of his mouth curving in amusement, and Claudia realised who he was.

'Roman Holidays,' she said flatly. 'You own a chain of sports shops.'

'Are you telling me or accusing me?' he asked, his eyes laughing at her. No wonder he could take time off whenever he pleased. Roman Holidays was highly successful world-wide. Her business was very small potatoes beside his empire.

'Come on, I'll drive you into Solihull,' he said, all traces of amusement banished.

'Not looking like this you won't! I must go home and change.' To her astonishment, he nodded curtly, and in a very short time they arrived at her flat.

He followed her in and she hurried into her bedroom, locked the door and took her time about showering and changing. Regretfully she decided not to wash her hair; it was so thick that it took ages to dry and she was sure his patience wouldn't last that long; also she had to get to work.

'A decided improvement,' he said, eyeing her pale green silk suit with favour. 'But I don't like the way you've done your hair.' He stretched out a hand and she stepped back hastily.

'I always wear it like this for work, so leave it alone.' He allowed his hand to drop.

'Very well—for now.' He strolled to the door, opening it for her, and she glanced at him crossly.

'Aren't you afraid I shall alert my neighbours?' she said as, taking her key, he locked the door behind them. 'One good scream and they'd phone the police. I don't think you'd find it easy to explain my torn blouse and dishevelled appearance, do you?'

A glint of admiration showed in his eyes, and before she could open her mouth she was in his arms and his mouth was on hers. It was more a punish-

ment than a kiss and she hated it, but she hated even
more the first faint stirring in her blood. He raised
his head and she thought he looked as dazed as she
felt, but the next moment she knew she had been
mistaken.

'So, you would cry rape, would you?' he snarled.
'And what would I be doing while you ruined that
pretty suit of yours?' Claudia bit her lip had.

'All right, so it wouldn't work, but what is
there——' She bit her tongue hard. What had got
into her? She had nearly told him she wouldn't be
there when he came for her.

'What's there to prevent you taking off to meet
Garry?' he asked, his tone the deceptive silk of a
thistle flower. Claudia made for the street, leaving
him to follow or not as he pleased.

He opened the car door for her; at least his
manners were good—it was a pity the rest of him
wasn't so nice. He drove smoothly into the town,
stopping before her shop.

'I like the name; it's a bit over-romantic, but I
suppose Dreams suits a business that sells wedding
dresses. In regard to your attempting to leave without me, that's up to you. I'm heartily tired of this
whole business. If it weren't for my sister I'd turn
the whole matter over to the police and let them find
Garry.' Claudia looked at him, her eyes wide.

'Hardly a matter for the police, is it?' she said,
wondering if his concern for Berenice had turned his
brain.

'Oh, didn't I tell you? Garry has diverted a
consignment of sports clothes to a friend of his and
we haven't been paid. It could be an oversight, but

it's enough for me to put the law on his trail.'
Claudia choked back a cry of dismay—he mustn't
do that. She had no doubt that Dana would be with
Garry and her twin wasn't made to stand up to that
kind of trouble.

'It would be a last resort but one I'll have to take
if I can't trace him soon.'

'He could be anywhere. . .you may never find
him.'

'That's possible—he knows I'll be looking for
him—but he'll have to remain in this country until
he can collect his legacy, and by then he'll expect
me to have given up.'

'He doesn't know you very well if he thinks that,'
she said faintly. Roman was the last man to turn
aside once he had decided on a course of action.
'What about me in all this?'

His mouth tightened into a hard line. 'Neither of
you will face criminal charges, though it would only
be justice after what you're doing to my sister. I
haven't contacted the police—yet—and if you co-
operate I may not have to trouble them. So it's in
your best interests to do exactly as I say, starting
now. Well?' as she didn't reply. 'Are you going to
arrange to be away for the next few days?'

'What about the show? Good as she is, Myra can't
handle that on top of everything else.'

'We'll come back for that if we haven't found
Garry by then. I also have clothes entered, so I need
to be there.'

'Back from where?' Claudia asked, hardly regis-
tering the rest of his words.

'That you will find out in due course; now go and make your arrangements and be ready by five.'

Claudia was greeted by concerned looks from Myra, who lost no time in following her into her office.

'What's all this about?' she said. 'Your Mr Wyatt says you need a holiday and, while I agree with him, it's not so simple, is it? Have you told him Dana is your twin?'

Claudia groaned and sank into her chair. 'I have, but he doesn't believe there are two of us; he saw the card you sent me and he thinks I got the idea of a twin from that. He also thinks I know where Garry might be, and he's determined to stay with me.'

'Could be exciting,' Myra said with a mischievous grin. 'Your Mr Wyatt is quite something. Do you know his birth sign?'

'No, I don't; you know I don't believe in anything like that.'

'I do,' Myra said, her eyes twinkling. Claudia raised her eyes to the ceiling.

'I know you do—why else would you devour the horoscopes in the daily paper and keep a book about it in your desk? But it's not for me. . .star signs and Mr Wyatt I can do without.'

'I'm not so sure about that, but I can see your problem. What are you going to do?'

'I have no choice other than to go along with him, for now anyway. If I refuse he'll set the police on to Garry, and think what that would do to Dana.'

'So there's more than just a missing husband,' Myra mused. 'I can see you'd want to be there if Dana was discovered with Garry,' she laughed. 'At least you'll have a break, and who knows what could happen? Men like Roman Wyatt don't appear every day.' She laughed again as Claudia said that once was too much, and from then on she treated Claudia as if she were going on holiday with the man of her dreams.

'I shall ring as often as I can, and if Dana phones try to get her address or telephone number,' Claudia said firmly, cutting across Myra's flight of fancy in which she and Roman Wyatt danced every night and forgot all about Dana and Garry.

Left alone in her office, Claudia signed letters to her supplies, wondering what Dana was doing and, more importantly, where she was. What would happen if and when they caught up with them? She had no doubt that, however long it took, Roman would find them. The head of a world-wide chain of shops, and goodness knew what else besides, wasn't going to stop before he reached his target. She dreaded to think how her twin would react.

Dana couldn't know about Berenice; she wasn't heartless. . .she wouldn't want a life built on another woman's misery. That was the one bright spot in the whole nasty business. As soon as she realised what Garry had done she would have nothing more to do with him.

If she really loved him she would be hurt badly at having to give him up, but there was no doubt in Claudia's mind what Dana would do. She, Claudia, would have to try to pick up the pieces, and that wouldn't be easy. Dana could seem ruthless; only her twin knew it was her inner insecurity that made

her present such a cold, unforgiving face to the
world.

The day ran by on swift feet and all too soon it
was five o'clock. Roman was early; Claudia left her
office on the hour, closing the door with an irrational
feeling that by the next time she saw it many things,
including herself, would be irrevocably changed. She
shook her head at her own lurid imagination and
walked into the showroom to find Roman examining
one of the dresses with critical eyes while Myra
chatted happily.

'This is excellent,' he said, turning to Claudia. 'It
wouldn't suit you, though; you need something
spectacular without being fussy.'

Myra laughed. 'Wait till the show—you've just
described the dress Claudia has designed and that
Dana will wear.' Claudia stole a look at him; he
didn't appear to have noticed Myra's saying Dana's
name. Just her luck; he would have believed Myra if
she had told him Claudia had a twin.

'You were saying, Myra, that Claudia is going to
model her own design in the show?' he said, his deep
voice startling both women.

'Myra said Dana is going to model the gown,'
Claudia said quickly.

'We all know, don't we, that you and Dana are
one?' he said scornfully. 'I applaud Myra's loyalty,
but it's stupid to carry on with this charade of twins.'
He looked at his slim gold wrist-watch and Claudia
shook her head at Myra's obvious intention of telling
him that Dana did exist. Nothing either of them
could say would convince Roman that she had a
twin.

'We should go—you still have to pack a case.'

'Don't forget to phone when you have the chance,' Myra said, shrugging her shoulders helplessly as Roman opened the door.

'We'll be in touch,' he said, and Claudia could have stamped her high heel on his foot. Myra's face was a study, and beneath her curls Claudia could almost see her brain making two and two equal a hundred. She had completely forgotten they were looking for Garry—she had them deep in a holiday romance.

'I wish you wouldn't give Myra ideas,' Claudia said irritably as they drove away from the showroom.

'I don't have to give your assistant ideas—she has enough of her own. I hadn't been in your shop two minutes before she asked me my birth date and told me her hobby is astrology.'

'It is,' Claudia said, momentarily diverted from her annoyance. 'She reads our horoscopes in the paper every day and firmly believes in them.'

'They have to fill the paper with something, but those things are about as real as this sister of yours.' Claudia scowled at him, refusing to say that Dana was real.

'I've told Myra you've mistaken me for Dana and that you're making me go with you to look for Garry, but she's inclined to discount that—she's building a romance round us.'

'Why have you told Myra about Garry? It doesn't resound to your credit, does it? I'd have thought you'd prefer the romantic idea.'

'I certainly do not. Myra has wedding bells ringing

in her ears all day; I don't want her to add me to her list of brides. Myra is a dear, but she's also a gossip. . .my reputation will be in shreds by the time I get back.'

'I wish your conscience worried you about my sister, but you're only concerned with yourself,' he said harshly.

'That's not true. I don't wish your sister any harm, but you should try to see my side of things.'

'I do. You're a mercenery bitch who puts her own interests before anything else.' Claudia caught back the angry words she wanted to hurl at him. It would do no good to tell him how hard she had worked to build her small business—he was too upset about his sister to listen.

His mouth was compressed into a straight line and his brows were drawn together. He was deeply worried about Berenice, and for a fleeting moment she was envious of the love he lavished on another woman.

She caught her breath—was she mad? She didn't even like him. He was an overbearing bastard; he was also sensitive to Berenice's distress. She sighed silently. Berenice was his sister; it was right he should be protective. It was also understandable that he should hate her for what he thought she was doing, or, rather, helping Garry do. It shouldn't hurt her that he despised her, but it did.

Roman brought the car to a halt in front of the flats and, without waiting for him to open her door, Claudia got out and inserted her key in the lock.

He was right behind her and there was no way she could keep him out.

'Pack a case and don't be long—jeans, tops, a dress or two and perhaps one formal outfit.' Claudia gave him a scornful look and made for the bathroom, taking a change of clothes with her. She hadn't the slightest idea where they were going, but the coffee knitted top and matching cotton trouser's teamed with a white jacket would be suitable for almost anything. She renewed her make-up, pausing as she met her blue eyes in the mirror.

What was she doing? She had always been the sensible, down-to-earth twin, yet here she was, going away with a man she had only known for two days.

'Dana, oh, Dana, what have you got me into?' she murmured to her reflection, but there was no answering twinge to say that Dana was aware of Claudia's distress. She turned away from the mirror and, putting her cosmetics in a vanity bag, opened the door.

Roman was in her bedroom, the contents of her dressing-table spread on the top. He glanced up as she came in and swept everything back into the drawer. Then, ignoring her indignant gasp, he made for the chest of drawers with the clear intention of searching that also.

'What do you think you're doing?' Claudia shot between him and the chest.

'Leave my things alone, or is that how you get your thrills, pawing women's underclothes?'

'I should slap you for that remark but you're not worth soiling my hands with. I'm looking for Garry's address.' He looked her over, insolently, from head to foot and, putting her to one side, opened the top drawer and pulled out a pair of silk camiknickers in a soft shade of amber.

'You'd look good in these, and even better without them,' he murmured. Claudia was so outraged that she had the greatest difficulty in keeping the rage she felt enough under control for her to be coherent. To her satisfaction, she managed very well.

'I thought you wouldn't soil your hands with me?' she asked silkily.

'I'd just like to look,' he said, and the picture he conjured up was so vivid that she felt heat rising to her face.

'So you can still blush,' he said. 'I find that remarkable.'

'Mr Wyatt, I don't have Garry Turner's address, and if I did I wouldn't keep it among my underwear,' she said desperately; the sight of her intimate things in his hands was sending strange shivers down her spine.

'No?' His eyes narrowed. 'Isn't that just the place a woman would keep her love letters, and Garry is the type of man who would write sweet nothings, isn't he?'

'You're not that type, I take it?'

'How right you are. You and I will have no need of letters *if* I decide to claim you.' Claudia held her ground with an effort. He couldn't mean she belonged to him—that would be the last thing either of them would want—but the predatory gleam in his eyes said differently, and an involuntary spark of anticipation was born deep inside her. It would be exciting to belong to a man like Roman; he would be no gentle lover. . .he would demand and give everything.

She turned away in confusion and started to pack a small case. He watched closely as she selected every garment, and at one point he took a dress from her, replacing it with another. She gave him a helpless look and meekly accepted the substitute. It wasn't one she would have chosen; she couldn't imagine what use a black lace evening dress would be, but then, she had no idea of where they were going. His presence was disturbing, to say the least of it, and she was relieved when, with an impatient, "hurry up", he strolled out of the room.

She walked into the sitting-room a few minutes later as he was replacing the phone.

'Berenice has given me a possible lead to her elusive husband.'

'What would that be?' Claudia said, trying to sound as if it were of no real interest to her.

'She's remembered she found a brochure for a hotel in Northumberland and she leapt to the conclusion that Garry was going to surprise her with an unexpected holiday. She thinks he's forgotten about it in the rush of leaving for America. I'd let her think his journey was an emergency. She's asked me to contact the hotel and cancel any booking he might have made.'

'You think Garry could be there?'

'Yes; I've just rung the hotel and a Mr and Mrs Smith are booked in—whether Garry is Mr Smith I don't know, but it's worth looking into.' Claudia's mind was working frantically.

'You must believe me now. I know nothing of any of this. Dana must be the Mrs Smith who's booked into that hotel.' His expression told her nothing had changed.

'Why should I believe you? Garry will have registered for you both and I'm sure he's eagerly awaiting your arrival.' Claudia felt thoroughly let down; she'd been so sure he would, at last, be convinced of the truth, and she hadn't realised how much she wanted him to think well of her until he had made it all too clear that he still didn't trust her. She put her disappointment to the back of her mind and concentrated on Dana.

If she could get the address or the telephone number of the hotel she could warn her twin that Roman knew where she and Garry were. She drifted slowly over to the telephone, most people doodled while they talked, and Roman proved no exception. There was a number on the pad; she tried to memorise it but a large hand was placed squarely on the pad.

'Clever girl, aren't you?' he said sarcastically. 'But it won't avail you of anything—I shan't allow you near a phone.'

'You can't be with me every moment,' she said defiantly.

'Want to bet?' he asked, so softly that she shivered.

'It will be impossible,' she returned, her spirited attack fading at his expression. He took the case from her and held the door open. She walked through, feeling like a condemned convict. He raised an eyebrow at the way she sat in the car, her feet together, her hands in her lap, her back stiff and her eyes looking straight ahead, a set expression on her face.

'Cheer up,' he said quietly. 'I'm not going to do anything you won't like.' That wasn't any comfort; part of the trouble, a big part, was that she could sympathise with him. She hated to think of his sister lying in hospital waiting for her husband to come to her while all the time he was with Dana.

She gripped her hands tightly together. Dana didn't know Berenice was in danger of losing her child; she was careless, but not vicious. Claudia made up her mind that she would help Roman as much as she could. She would also find a way to protect her twin—after all, it wasn't a crime to run away with the man you loved.

'I'm very sorry about your sister, Mr Wyatt,' she said stiffly, 'but why not wait until your brother-in-law comes back of his own accord?' His hands tightened on the steering-wheel.

'Berenice needs him now. She won't believe he can't get to a phone for much longer. I don't like lying to my sister, and I've now run out of tales she'll believe.' He looked at her shrewdly. 'If I did wait for Garry to come back into the fold, what would you be doing?'

'I should abandon this farce of a holiday and go home to attend to my business. What else would I do?'

'Make a time and place to meet your lover,' he sneered. 'You have a low opinion of my intelligence if you think I'd let you get away with that.' She

turned her head to look at him. He was nobody's
fool, but she had to try, for Dana's sake.

'It's time you called me Roman—we're going to
be very close to each other until we find Garry, and
it won't do for you to address me as Mr Wyatt.'

'Why not? It's how I think of you,' she said, the
hated colour rising to her face as she uttered the lie.
She had thought of him as Roman since the first
moment she had known his name.

'It's not a difficult one,' he returned mildly. 'Say
it, Claudia.' He put one hand on her thigh.
'Claudia,' he warned, and, shrinking from the heat
of his hand which burned through her trousers like a
red-hot iron, she stammered his name.

'Again, louder.'

'Roman, Roman—there, does that satisfy you?'

'No, did you think it would?'

Claudia rushed into speech, unable to understand
why his reply should send her mind into erotic
overdrive. 'Roman is an unusual Christian name,'
she said, wishing and dreading that he would remove
his hand.

'My mother was Italian; it means a man from
Rome. Claudia and Roman go well together, don't
they? I'm sure we would be equally as good as a
pair.'

Claudia lost her breath; this was intolerable—not
only had she been forced to accompany him on a
wild chase after Garry Turner, but she was being
subjected to what amounted to sexual harassment.
She lifted his hand from her leg and placed it on the
steering-wheel, surprised that he showed no
resistance.

'It's dangerous to drive with only one hand on the wheel, and I object to your touching me.'

'You should have said something before this. I wouldn't want you to be nervous, but I like touching you. You have a beautiful skin, soft and lustrous, even if it is covered up.'

'That doesn't give you the right to make free with me whenever you choose. Keep away, or I'll— I'll——'

'You'll what—surrender without protest?'

'Certainly not. You're the last man I would——'

'Make love with? I think you're protesting too much.'

'Aren't you forgetting you think I'm your brother-in-law's woman?' she said, shrinking from him as he turned a look of such anger on her that she shuddered.

'It's a good thing for you I'm driving or I might just show you whose woman you really are. As it is, thank you for reminding me.'

'Where are we going?' she asked some time later. She had assumed they were going to his friend's colourful flat but they had been on the motorway for several miles and the road signs said they were travelling north.

'We're going to Northumberland, but it has been an exhausting few days for me and I intend to stop halfway. I need a good night's sleep before confronting Garry.'

He sounded so confident that she started to panic. How could she warn Dana? She could only pray that Dana had come to her senses and had left before they arrived at Garry's hide-out. Hide-out. . .what a description; he had her thinking like an old film now.

'Don't you think you're taking this a bit too far? Garry's an adult, and if he and your sister can't live together it could be best for her if he does leave.'

'I think you're forgetting my sister's condition,' he said heavily. Claudia's hands flew to her throat; for a moment that was just what she had done. How cold she have been so callous as to forget Berenice's unborn baby?

CHAPTER FOUR

THEY left the motorway at the next junction, and the busy road gave way to the outskirts of a small town.

'We're nearing Kendal,' Roman said. 'There's a motel here, and this is as far as I want to drive today.' Claudia was too anxious to say anything; a night here would give her the chance to phone Dana and end this farce. Roman exclaimed in satisfaction and, turning into a wide drive, pulled up in front of a building that said it was a motor halt.

'Not very imaginative, and I don't expect the accommodation will be marvellous, but it will do for one night.' He got out and strode into the reception office without waiting for her. She followed, trying to spot a public phone, and she had just caught sight of one at the corner of the building when he came out of the office, a key in his hand.

He took her arm, put her deftly back into the car and drove round to where small cottages nestled among trees.

'Number twenty-six,' he said, parking neatly before a compact cottage. Claudia followed him in a daze. It seemed a long time since Dana's phone call had brought Roman Wyatt into her life and she badly needed to be by herself to think about the turmoil he had caused in her ordered existence. She glanced at her watch and was astonished to see it was nearly nine o'clock—no wonder she was tired and hungry.

'This is adequate—just,' he said, and she came to life.

'It will be fine for me. What number is your room?'

Roman chuckled. 'This is the only room available—we have to share. I assure you, I'm a good bed-mate.'

'I'm not sharing with you,' Claudia said, her eyes darting, from one single bed to the other. 'One of us will have to sleep in the car.'

'That would start people talking—husbands and wives usually sleep together.'

'Husbands and wives. . .oh, no, you didn't sign us in as a married couple?'

'Why not? It saves a lot of questions.' He put his hands on her shoulders, stopping her from running to the door. 'I don't force my attentions on any woman, and you are doubly safe. If I were to get carried away with desire for your beautiful body the remembrance that you are Garry's woman would act as a cold shower.' Claudia drew a shaky breath. Could she trust him? But then, she had little choice; he wouldn't allow her to sleep in the car or to remain here without him.

'I have to take your word that you'll leave me alone?' she asked tautly, tilting her head in enquiry.

'You do, and now we'll get something to eat. There's a café on the site, and luckily it stays open late, so come along.' Claudia went along, his manner more than his words warning her he wasn't about to stand any nonsense.

Less than an hour later they were back in number

twenty-six, and she was so tired that she was past worrying about having to sleep in the same room but, confronted by the reality of the limited space, two small beds and a very large, powerful man, her nervous fears came back like a river in full spate. She stood by the door like a small animal poised for flight, and Roman uttered an irritable exclamation.

'I'm not going to pounce. I'm far too tired, even if I were at all tempted. You can have the bathroom first. It has a good lock in case my lust for your luscious body gets the better of me.'

He sounded so disgusted that she seized her case and bolted through the door he indicated. After what he'd said she didn't dare turn the key in the lock, but she made short work of undressing. She opened the case and looked with dismay at the flimsy green silk nightdress lying on top of the matching gown.

She couldn't remember packing that. A picture of Roman handing her things and taking others from her came into her mind. Her sensible cotton night-shirt must have been one of his discards.

She pulled the nightdress over her head. It was one of her own designs, but whether she would ever have worn it, if it hadn't been for the interfering Roman Wyatt, she didn't know. A bang on the door galvanised her into action; she gathered the matching gown round her and opened the door.

'About time,' he said, his eyes taking in the picture she made. She tried to slide past him but he swung round with her, catching both her hands and holding her in front of him.

'I'm beginning to understand why Garry went overboard for you,' he said huskily.

'He didn't,' Claudia said hotly.

'I believe you,' he said unexpectedly. 'Garry panicked at the thought of responsibility and, if I read your character rightly, you didn't know anything about Berenice except for her existence. I'd like to think that, if you had known, you wouldn't be prepared to join her husband, but that would be stretching credulity too far.'

'I'd like to point out that I am not Dana and I am with you, not Garry,' she said, flicking her tongue across dry lips. Roman's eyes gleamed and she pulled away, backing nervously until stopped by a bed.

'Go to bed, for goodness' sake,' he snarled. 'You have nothing to fear from me, even in that outfit. You look the model for all virginal brides, and I'm beginning to wish I'd let that awful shroud remain in your case.' He slammed into the bathroom and Claudia jumped into the nearest bed and pulled the covers under her chin.

She couldn't relax; she could hear every move he made through the flimsy wall, and each one stretched her nerves tight. The door opened and she held her breath as she sensed him standing by her bed, releasing it as she heard the creak of the other bed.

The covers rustled and her tightly held muscles loosened a bit, only to clench tightly again as he chuckled.

'Relax, Claudia, I'm too tired to do you justice, so you're quite safe—for the moment.'

* * *

Claudia came awake slowly, the smell of coffee tantalising her nostrils. She opened her eyes, a gasp of alarm escaping her at the sight of Roman, dressed in black trousers and a black cotton shirt, standing by her bed.

'What time is it?' she asked, berating herself for having slept all night. She had meant to wait until he was asleep before slipping out to phone Dana, but the long, nerve-racking day had caught up with her.

'It's eight o'clock, and as soon as we've had breakfast we'll be on our way.' He handed her a mug and she raised an eyebrow.

'I'm perfectly capable of making a cup of coffee,' he said drily, reading her expression with an ease that made her uncomfortable. 'Drink up and get dressed. We'll have breakfast in the café we used last night. Don't hang about,' he said impatiently as she stared at him, the bedclothes clutched tightly round her. 'I'll give you fifteen minutes; then I'm coming back in,' he said, putting his head round the door just as she threw back the covers. 'I wouldn't get any ideas about running if I were you,' he said, looking her over as if he were contemplating buying. 'I shall be just outside.'

Claudia gulped the coffee, feeling she needed something to offset Roman's razor-sharp mind. He was several steps ahead of her all the time and outwitting him would need a genius, and that she wasn't.

She dressed in black trousers and a white blouse with long full sleeves, brushed her hair till it shone and twisted it into a tight knot on top of her head, thinking with satisfaction that Roman wouldn't like

it but she wasn't about to let him dictate how she
wore her hair, or dressed.

She folded her nightgown and robe, pushing them
into a corner of her case without regard for the
fragile material. He hadn't done a bad job of dictat-
ing her actions so far but that didn't mean it had to
continue. The door opened as she was counting her
change and he looked suspiciously at the coins in her
palm.

'Going somewhere?' he asked politely; the quiet
voice held hidden traps, warning her that the answer
had better be in the negative.

'How could I even think of it when you dog my
every step? For your information, I want to phone
Myra.'

'Afraid your business will fall to pieces without
you?'

'It's a small business and, though Myra is good,
the responsibility rests with me.' He looked at her
thoughtfully for a long moment before nodding.

'Very well, there's a phone by the reception. You
can phone now.' Claudia followed him, wondering if
he was going to crowd into the phone box with her,
but he remained outside and she dialled Dana's
number, her heart beating wildly. The phone rang
on and on, but just as she was about to give up she
was answered by a sleepy female voice.

'Can I speak to Dana, please?' Claudia asked,
knowing the answer before the other woman spoke.
'Tell her it's Claudia.'

'Oh, Dana's goody-goody sister——Oops,
shouldn't have said that.' There was a giggle, and
Claudia clung on to the phone, feeling faint.

'Can I speak to Dana?' she asked again, pain at the way Dana had described her swamped by her anxiety to speak to her sister.

'I'm Norma, Dana's flatmate, but she's not here; she's gone off with her lover-boy—I don't know where.'

'If she phones you will you ask her to contact Myra at the showroom, please?' Claudia said. Her hopes had been lifted high; now she felt numb.

'Will do,' Norma said and put the phone down, leaving Claudia feeling she would forget all about her request within seconds.

She dialled Myra's number and it was answered at once. Myra's familiar voice made her want to cry; it seemed such a long time since things had been normal, with nothing more exciting than new orders to think about.

'Hello,' Myra said again, and Claudia managed to answer, asking her to do everything she could to get an address or phone number if Dana got in touch with her.

'I certainly will, but enough about Dana,' Myra answered. 'I'm much more interested in you and Mr Wyatt. I looked his birth date up after you'd gone, and he's a Sagittarius.' She sounded as if Claudia would know what she was talking about.

'A Sagittarius,' Claudia said, wondering what that had to do with anything.

'Yes,' Myra said patiently. 'They're depicted as a Centaur, half-man, half-horse.' Claudia groaned; that information she could do without. Roman as a man was bad enough, but a Centaur?

'Sagittarians and Geminis go well together, in all

ways,' Myra said, her voice loaded with significance.
'You have a unique opportunity to explore his
character and everything else—don't waste it,
Claudia,' she added slyly.

'I'll ignore that last bit, Myra; all I want to do is
get this apology for a holiday over and get back to
work.' She went on to talk about the shop, giving
Myra no time to say anything else about Roman.
The door of the phone box opened, giving her the
chance she wanted to break off and, cutting short
Myra's eager question, she stepped out of the box
almost into Roman's embrace. She stifled an exclamation as he took her roughly by her wrists.

'Who did you phone besides Myra?' he asked, a
glint in his eyes saying it would be no use denying it.

'I tried to phone Dana, but she's left her flat,'
Claudia said, too weary of the whole thing to say
anything except the truth.

'So we're back to your imaginary twin, are we?'
Roman said, his mouth curling with distaste. 'I could
almost think she were real if I didn't know better,
but unfortunately for you and your tales my detective is an expert. He wouldn't miss a thing like that.'

'He did miss it; it's a pity you didn't hear me
asking Dana's flatmate for her—you'd have had to
believe me then.' Roman's look of disgust deepened.

'I don't think so; you and Myra are quite capable
of trying to mislead me. I don't trust you and I shall
be breathing down your neck next time you pick up
a phone.'

'Where are we going?' Claudia asked as they
left the motel behind them. 'You mentioned
Northumberland, but which part?'

'The hotel is in Alnwick, so that's where we're heading. If Garry is there we can be back home very shortly, and you can go back to your wedding dresses.'

'It was very careless of your brother-in-law to leave that brochure lying about. Are you sure it wasn't a surprise for Berenice?'

'I'm sure it wasn't; Garry isn't the brightest of men; he'd deceive himself into thinking I wouldn't try to trace him, and if it weren't for my sister I wouldn't bother; the discrepancies in the accounts would be compensated for by his permanent absence from the firm.' He fell silent, thinking, Claudia had no doubt, of his sister and how badly she needed her husband.

'Even if you do find him, you can't make him go back to your sister,' she said slowly.

'I think I can. I didn't say his manipulation of the accounts weren't serious—they are—but I'm prepared to let them go if Garry toes the line.' Claudia breathed out audibly. Men hadn't a bit of sense when it came to personal relationships.

'What good will that do? The last thing your sister wants is an unwilling husband.'

'I agree,' he said, to her surprise, 'but until the baby is safely born she needs Garry at her side, and that's where he'll be if I have anything to do with it.'

'After the baby comes, what then?'

Roman's expresion darkened. 'I'm hoping the child will compensate Berenice for the loss of her husband, and who knows? He could have a change of heart and settle down to family life.'

Claudia sat quietly beside him as he turned off the

main road. The scenery was fascinating; mountains
were beginning to appear in the distance, beckoning
to her with a blue, misty enchantment, to which she
responded with a longing she couldn't believe she
possessed.

'I've never been to Northumberland before,' she
said wistfully. Roman shot her a glance that told her
nothing of what he was thinking.

'It's not all that far from the Midlands.'

'I know, but my mother liked the south coast and
London for holidays, and Dad just went along; if it
suited Mother it suited him.'

'An ideal marriage,' he replied, his tone saying
there was no such thing. Claudia smiled wryly; her
parents' marriage had been peaceful, mainly because
both parents went their own way, each, figuratively,
taking one child with them.

The hum of the tyres on the road lulled her into a
doze that deepend into a sound sleep. She surfaced
as the car slowed down and turned sharply to the
right. She sat up and rubbed her eyes, colouring
furiously as she realised she had been using Roman's
shoulder for a head-rest.

'I'm sorry; I didn't mean to fall asleep and use you
as a pillow.' She was taken by surprise by the
friendly smile he turned on her, and for a moment
she dreamed they were going on a holiday together
that had nothing to do with Dana and Garry and
everything to do with each other.

'I rather like your head on my shoulder,' he said
quietly. 'Though we're wearing too many clothes,
and a bed would be preferable to a car.' The veils of
sleep and illusion dropped away and she moved as

far away from him as the seatbelt allowed, turning her face to the window.

The small town of Alnwick was bustling with people, and Roman drove through the crowded streets slowly.

'I'm looking for the Crowned Head,' he said. 'Keep a watch on your side.' After a moment he exclaimed in satisfaction and swung the car into a narrow lane.

Claudia had just time to see a sign in gold and red before they turned into a cobbled yard. She got out of the car, dreading the moment when she would have to meet Dana. Her sister would blame Claudia for tracking her down; she wouldn't believe she'd had little choice in the matter.

Roman grasped her arm, pulling her with him into the hotel. He strode to the reception desk, holding her firmly at his side, and she looked fearfully round, half expecting Dana to appear. Roman asked the receptionist for Garry's room number and Claudia saw the girl's polite manner deepen to one of appreciation of the man in front of her.

'Mr Smith's room is number fifty-six, but he and Mrs Smith have joined a coach party touring the Roman wall and they won't be back until tomorrow afternoon,' the girl said with a warm smile at Roman. Claudia smiled wryly, acknowledging that Roman would always receive this kind of reaction from every woman he met. Roman thanked the girl and asked her not to tell Mr Smith he had been asking for him.

'He thinks I'm out of the country and we'd like to surprise him, wouldn't we, darling?' He curled his

arm round Claudia's waist, smiling at the receptionist in a way that made her assure him she would
keep his secret.

She would too; there were very few women who
could resist charm like that. She had no time for
further reflection as he marched her smartly out of
the hotel and back to the car.

'Where are we going now?' she asked as he swung
the car back into the main street.

'To our hotel. You didn't think I intended to stay
at the Crowned Head, did you?' Claudia shook her
head; she hadn't thought beyond seeing Dana.
Dana; she was the Mrs Smith the girl had referred
to. At last Roman would know she had spoken the
truth when she'd denied knowing Garry. He glanced
at her and she was surprised to see warmth in his
eyes before he concentrated on the road ahead.

He turned the car into a narrow street and stopped
in a yard that could have been the twin of the one at
the other hotel. This hotel looked older and rejoiced
in the name of the Lion's Cub. Claudia looked at
him in enquiry as he opened the door.

'Come on, I'd like a drink and something to eat.
We'll register first, then find some food.' The young
man behind the desk smiled in response to Roman's
query, uttered in too low a tone for Claudia to hear.

Roman signed the register the man handed him
and, telling him to send the luggage up, took
Claudia's arm, and they were out in the street before
she could speak.

'Shouldn't I have signed the register?' she said,
not at all sure she liked his high-handed manner.

'I signed for you; it's not important, and I'm too

hungry to argue.' She was also hungry, very hungry, she acknowledged a short time later as she did justice to the duckling and fresh vegetables Roman had ordered.

'That's better; now I suggest we try to forget why we're here and play tourist for the rest of the day.' He looked at her, his amber eyes sparkling. 'Well, do you agree?'

Claudia considered his offer for a moment and found she was smiling and agreeing to his suggestion.

'Good.' He summoned the waiter and, with the speed she was getting used to, paid the bill, and they left the restaurant, his hand on her arm.

The afternoon passed by in such a confusion of sights and sounds that she thought she would never remember any of them. It was also fun. Roman was a good companion when he set his mind to it.

She clutched his arm at one point, bringing him to a halt in the middle of the pavement, heedless of the passers-by as she pointed to a tall column at the end of the street.

'What's that?' she asked. 'Why is a lion perched high above the town, and why is his tail standing straight out like that?' Roman laughed, his musical chuckle making her laugh in her turn.

'I don't know why his tail is like that, but the Percy Lion was erected to the lord of the manor by his tenants in gratitude for his leniency with their rents in a time of hardship. Unfortunately for the farmers, their lord and master thought they must be more prosperous than they'd led him to believe, and he promptly put the rents back up.'

'Oh, dear, what a shame when they were only

trying to show their appreciation.' Claudia's smile vanished and she blinked away a tear at the thought of the poor farmers who had been so misunderstood.

'It was a long time ago,' Roman said softly, slipping his arm round her waist and holding her against him as they walked.

'I'm being silly.'

'Not silly, just compassionate,' he murmured, his mouth close to her ear. Claudia moved briskly away from him by dodging a small girl who was eating an ice-cream. Roman frowned and she knew he was angry at her manoeuvre, but he was far too fond of holding her close to him on any excuse, and she was finding his touch more and more disturbing.

'Time for tea,' Roman said, replacing his arm round her waist and steering her into a nearby café. Claudia sighed in resignation. He had decided to act as if they liked each other; he didn't know how he affected her and he wasn't going to know. She would just have to find some way of avoiding physical contact until Dana returned from her trip to Hadrian's Wall.

She sat down at the table for two Roman had selected, and tossed her hair back from her face; Roman had pulled the pins out as soon as they had left the hotel and placed them in his pocket. She met his determined gaze and knew that avoiding him wasn't going to be easy. He hadn't got where he was in the world without knowing how to get what he wanted, and he appeared to want her.

No, of course he didn't—how foolish could she get? He thought she was Garry's lover, and he was the last man to want another man's discarded lover.

She felt a sharp pang at the thought that he couldn't possibly desire her, and scolded herself for feeling like that. He was a self-opinionated, overbearing tyrant, and he was the last man she should want to tangle with. He also cared deeply for his sister, and their afternoon together had proved he had a sense of humour and could be a considerate and friendly companion.

Claudia drank her tea, refusing any of the cakes she was offered, watching him as he devoured several with enjoyment.

'I have a sweet tooth,' he said blandly as he disposed of the fourth.

'So I see,' she said, laughing at his sheepish small-boy expression. After they left the café they wandered round the town for a while longer, but Claudia began to feel very weary. She longed for a shower and a rest, to say nothing of a change of clothes.

'Back to the hotel; you look a bit wilted,' Roman said bluntly, and Claudia scowled.

'Whose fault is that? I've been on the go all day. I need a shower and a short rest.'

'You shall have both,' he promised, and within a very short time they were back in the blissfully cool hotel. He strode to the desk while Claudia waited listlessly by the lift.

'We're on the top floor,' he said, urging her into the lift. Claudia accepted his arm round her shoulders as inevitable; she was far too tired to fight him at the moment.

The lift came to a halt and Roman practically lifted her into a quiet corridor with only one door opening from it.

'The penthouse suite,' he announced and, inserting a key into the lock, opened the door and swept her with him into the spacious sitting-room. Claudia turned to run, fear breaking through her fatigue. The devil had booked them into the same room.

'Hold it,' he commanded sharply, catching her before she could reach the door. 'I said a suite; there are two bedrooms, though if you want to spare the maids some work we can share.'

'I won't share anything with you,' she said as calmly as she could. 'Contrary to anything you may think, I have a regard for my reputation.'

'All taken care of,' he said smoothly. 'I registered us as Mr and Mrs Wyatt.' Claudia stared at him blankly, unable to take it in for several minutes, and when she did she cried out and launched herself at him, her hands raised. He caught her easily, holding both wrists in one hand and bringing her hard against him. He put his other arm round her waist and she thought wildly that it could make its own way there by now.

'I don't advise you to hit me, Claudia; I shall retaliate, but I won't hit you,' he said as alarm flared in her blue eyes. 'There are other ways to control you, ways far more pleasurable than a blow.' He lowered his head, closing his mouth over hers; his lips were warm and firm and his tongue tantalised her firmly closed mouth.

Claudia gave up without a struggle to the sensations that were shaking her slender form. She lifted her arms to his shoulders and ran her fingers through his crisp hair, shivering at the silken touch.

Roman growled softly in satisfaction, his lips

demanding she should kiss him in return. Claudia's heart thudded fiercely and she felt Roman's heart quicken in response. His hand closed over her breast and she parted her lips in answer to his silent command.

'You make me want you,' he murmured. Claudia trembled. . .she wanted him as much, but this wasn't right; Roman despised her, he thought she was taking Garry from his wife, and there was no way they could take this any further. She stiffened, letting her arms fall to her sides, and he raised his head, looking at her with eyes that glittered with anger.

'What's the matter, Claudia—just realised I'm not Garry?' He stepped away from her and she could have wept at the cold desolation that closed round her.

'You still can't believe I have anything to do with Garry—he's with Dana. Who else do you think Mrs Smith is?'

His glance contained both pity and rejection. 'You have been thrown over for another woman, that's what I think. If it's your sister that must be doubly hurtful, but I'm still not convinced of her existence.' Claudia could have cried; how stubborn could he get?'

'You still think I'm Garry's mistress?' she asked quietly.

'I would like to think otherwise but——' He held his hands out in denial. Claudia's face mirrored her distress and he pulled her to him. 'It must be torture to be betrayed by your sister,' he said quietly.

'Then you do believe she exists?' Claudia said eagerly.

'It seems she does; you wouldn't persist in a story that will be disproved as soon as I meet Mr and Mrs Smith, but I don't believe you're identical twins. I can understand your outrage at your sister taking your place; what I don't see is why you persist in denying your own relationship with Garry.'

'It's useless for me to try to answer you.' Claudia was so exhausted that she could hardly remain upright.

'I'll never know what you women see in Garry,' Roman growled. 'First my sister, then you, and now this new woman. What has he got that we lesser men have not?'

'I've not the slightest idea,' Claudia said, turning to face him. He looked tired and upset and her heart went out to him. He had the worry and responsibility of his sister on his shoulders, and she wished she could take him in her arms and comfort him.

'I'm not one of Garry's women. One day perhaps you will believe me. In the meantime, if you are still determined to keep me here, could we try not to fight?'

'A truce. . .do you think it will work?'

'Perhaps not, but I'm too tired to quarrel at the moment.' She held out her hand and he looked at her, his amber eyes serious, before taking her in his arms.

His kiss was deep and sensual; she opened her mouth without hesitation, moulding herself against

him eagerly. She didn't remember that only minutes
before he had accused her of being another man's
discarded woman. She only knew she wanted to get
as close to him as she could.

CHAPTER FIVE

CLAUDIA was drowning in a sea of sensations so strong that she wanted to rip away the clothes that kept them apart. She wanted to feel Roman's skin against her and his hands on her naked body. She was utterly shocked when he put her firmly from him and she saw him button the shirt she had succeeded in undoing.

'I have to hand it to you,' he said grimly, 'you lose one lover and waste no time in replacing him. That I have much more of this world's goods than Garry will ever have couldn't help you to that decision, could it?' he said, and her heart sank at the cynical twist to his mouth and his bitter tone.

'Your money, or lack of it, has nothing to do with anything,' she said coldly, holding her trembling hands tightly together behind her back.

'You must excuse me if I don't believe you,' he sneered. 'My experience with women leads me to think differently.' Claudia looked at him curiously; he sounded as if some woman had hurt him badly, but surely not. Roman wasn't the type to lose control over any woman, and he was so powerfully attractive that she couldn't imagine any woman turning him down.

'That truce didn't last long, did it? I don't think we should try another one, do you?'

'I wouldn't say that; I think we could practise an armistice in the right place.'

'That place being your bed?'

'How quick and how right you are; we could deal very well together—you'll find I am a generous lover, as long as you understand I'm not walking up the aisle with you, or any other woman.'

'Someone must have hurt you very much,' Claudia said, her voice warm with sympathy. He sent her a look of disgust.

'Why do women always think another woman is behind a man's decision to remain free?'

'Because she usually is. I'm not trying to pry, Roman—or not very much,' she added honestly as his lips twisted in a cynical smile.

'No? You're just feeling sorry for me. You'll be offering to be a sister with a shoulder I can cry on in a moment, won't you? Well, I don't want your sympathy, and I don't want you as a sister—I already have more than I can handle in that department, thank you.'

'I'm not offering anything else,' she said, her voice thickening at the thought of what anything else could be.

'Pity, or is it? You're still too near to Garry for my taste.' He raised a hand in an expressive gesture. 'You're quite safe; I shall not be invading your room tonight.' He opened one of the doors and waved her through.

'Choose your room, Claudia; they're both about the same, I expect.' Claudia glanced round at the cream and green furnishings, noting the comfortable double bed before opening the other door. As he had said, they were identical except that this room was in cream and brown.

'I'll have the first one; it's only for one night, anyway.'

'Bathroom through here—afraid we have to share.' He carried her case into the room she had chosen and she caught her breath as their eyes met. The room revolved round her and she ran her tongue over suddenly dry lips. Roman's eyes followed the movement, his eyes darkened, and the tension between them increased to danger point. Claudia raised a hand to her throat and the gesture broke the spell.

'Dinner in half an hour? I think we'll try the restaurant here; I don't think it would be a good idea to have room service, do you?' Claudia drew a deep breath; she agreed with him wholeheartedly. She wasn't hungry—her appetitite had disappeared during the long moments she had looked into his amber eyes. He wanted her badly, and if he'd taken her in his arms she didn't think she would have put up any kind of resistance.

'Here will be fine,' she said huskily, relieved she could speak at all. He nodded and closed the door behind him. She listened for the click of his door and relaxed when it came, only to be aware of every sound he made.

This was madness. Roman Wyatt was way out of her league; he was a high-powered business tycoon with beautiful women falling over themselves for a glance from his magnificent eyes. He wouldn't look twice at a small-town girl, even if she could design wedding dresses.

To add to that, he hated her for what he thought she was doing to his sister. He was attracted to her, as any red-blooded male would be to any presentable woman in these circumstances, but that was as far as it went and it was up to her to make sure her own feelings didn't betray her.

She opened her case and unpacked with unnecessary vigour. She mustn't lose sight of why she was here. Dana had to be shielded from Roman's anger, and she was the only one who could do that.

She paused. Dana was an adult. What reason had she to think her twin needed protection? She picked up a cotton skirt patterned with roses. She felt responsible for Dana, but why did she? Did she feel guilty because she and Dana weren't as close as twins usually were?

Dana didn't need her care—on the contrary, she showed only too clearly that she resented her twin's interference. Claudia started to undress. Roman had said half an hour and he was quite capable of walking in on her if she was late. She stood under the shower, her thoughts going back to Dana.

Why had she never realised before this that Dana had every right to do as she pleased, regardless of how her sister felt? She turned off the shower and reached for a towel. Stupid she might be to try to protect her sister, but old habits clung and she couldn't abandon Dana to Roman's anger.

She tried to ignore the feeling that she didn't want to leave him by telling herself that she must be there if Dana needed her. She pulled on her gown, unaware of how the thin silk clung to her still-damp skin.

A door she had thought led to a cupboard opened, and Roman came in. He was naked except for a pair of shorts and a white towelling robe, draped over one shoulder, emphasising the strength of his bronze chest. He smiled and she pulled her robe tightly round her; the bathroom that had seemed quite large had shrunk to the few feet between them.

'Are you coming or going?' he enquired silkily, and Claudia shivered. Like his smile, his tone sent waves of excitement coursing through her. 'I hope you're coming—we can share a shower to save water. I'm sure you're keen on conservation, aren't you?'

She sent him a haunted look, stammered that she was going, and tried to sidle past him. He moved, pressing her between the shower and his hard masculine body. Claudia panicked and, lifting her hands, tried to push him away. It was a mistake; her gown fell open, and he went very still, his eyes leaping with fire as he devoured the slender form in front of him.

'Please, let me pass; I want to get dressed.' She clutched at the thin gown, but he caught her hands, pulling them apart.

'Not yet,' he said thickly, and fire ran through her veins as his hands cupped her breasts, making her gasp at the surge of pleasure his fingers evoked.

'You're so beautiful, how can you be so callous of another woman's unhappiness when you look like an angel direct from heaven?'

'I'm not callous; if I could help your sister I would,' she murmured, hardly aware of what either of them was saying. She swayed towards him, wanting to feel his skin against hers, but his mood changed as swiftly as the wind and he pulled the gown round her roughly, his eyes as cold as stones.

'You're a liar and a hypocrite, that you're also Garry's discarded lover doesn't absolve you from the guilt of taking him from Berenice in the first place.'

'I don't suppose "Mrs Smith" is the first woman with whom Garry has deceived his wife, and she probably won't be the last,' she said, her desire for him disappearing at the contempt in his tone.

'She will, if he knows where his best interests lie. His legacy won't last forever, and I'm prepared to overlook a good many faults, business-wise, for my sister's sake.' He stared at her intently and she felt her face grow warm.

'Remarkable—you can still blush,' he said again sarcastically, and she blushed harder than ever. 'I can't understand why Garry would want another woman when he has you,' he said, and Claudia groaned.

'Can't you admit you might have made a mistake?'

'After the photographs I showed you? And they weren't the only ones. Some of the others were more, shall we say, explicit. No, my dear Claudia, I haven't made a mistake; the mistake is Garry's; whoever his new woman is, she can't be as lovely as you are.'

'Garry may see things differently.'

'You don't seem very upset. I expected you to dissolve into tears at the thought of your lover with another woman.' Claudia sent him an irritated look and edged past him. She wasn't going to protest her innocence again, but it was time this scene with its explosive potential was ended. Roman let her go and she closed the door on him with relief, pushing any tinge of regret that he hadn't kissed her firmly away.

She dressed quickly in a slim cream silk dress that had no ornament at all, relying for its impact on the way it followed the curves of her body, gently touching and emphasising full breasts, narrow waist and the flare of her hips.

The thirty minutes Roman had allowed her had just ended when he came into the sitting-room. Claudia, standing by the window, looking down at the street, knew the moment he stepped over the threshold. She turned round slowly and her heart missed a beat. Dressed in well-cut silver-grey trousers and a pale green shirt, open at the neck, a grey jacket slung casually over one shoulder, he could have stepped out of every woman's dream.

'If you continue to look at me like that we shan't make it any further than the nearest bed,' he murmured, and Claudia jumped; she had been staring at him hungrily.

'Blushing again?' he said, trailing a finger down her hot cheek and across her mouth. 'I would dearly love to know your thoughts. Won't you share them with me?'

'No, I won't. You might have made me come on this asburd chase, but what I think is my business.'

'It will be mine soon; I'll have all of you. . .your every thought will be open to me, as mine will be to you. No, don't bother to voice the protest I see forming on your beautiful lips; it will happen sooner or later, but I agree with you that we must get this business of Garry cleared up first.

'Once he is back with Berenice, and this latest "Mrs Smith" has gone back to whichever hole she crawled out of, we'll have all the time in the world for our own affairs.'

'Do you still think I'm Mrs Smith?' Claudia demanded.

'Obviously you're not—this time—but I still think you've been involved with Garry in the past. My detective has been very inefficient. I can't understand why he didn't know you weren't the only woman in Garry's life.' He looked at her, a puzzled, uncertain expression on his face.

'You are the last woman I would have thought I would want—you're everything I despise, but you're in danger of becoming an obsession and there's only one way to deal with it: we'll make love until we're sated with each other, then we'll both be free to go our separate ways and forget we ever met.'

'I like the forgetting bit, but you can forget anything else—you're the last man I'd ever make love with.'

He smiled, and Claudia thought that, if tigers could smile, that was what it would be like.

'Protest and wriggle all you like; the end result isn't in doubt. Now dinner awaits us, unless you're going to change your mind about having it here, on our own.' His words opened a door through which she refused to go, and she swept past him, her head high, hearing him chuckle as if she amused him.

* * *

Claudia closed the door of her room, turning the key firmly in the lock. Dinner had been surprisingly relaxed and friendly. They had talked about Northumberland—or, rather, Roman had talked and she had listened, at first apathetically, but gradually, as he'd spoken about the Romans, she'd become more and more fascinated.

They had continued their conversation after dinner, sitting in the comfortable bar. Claudia sipped white wine while Roman demonstrated the layout of a Roman fort with his brandy glass and ashtrays gathered from adjoining tables.

She was so interested that she was only vaguely aware the room was emptying of other guests until a waiter picked up their empty glasses and obstinately replaced the ashtrays Roman had borrowed.

'Do you think he's trying to tell us something?' Roman said, quirking an eyebrow. He grinned at her expression and, taking her hand, pulled her to her feet.

'Bedtime—you look as if you'll fall asleep where you sit at any moment. I must have bored you out of your mind.'

'Nothing of the kind,' Claudia said indignantly. Roman chuckled, and she knew he had got the reaction he had wanted. 'Honestly, I was very interested; I've never thought much about the Roman invasion, but you bring it to life.'

'It's a pity we haven't time to visit the wall on this trip,' Roman said as they entered their suite. 'Berenice will come first, but we'll come again and I shall take pleasure in seeing it through your eyes.' Claudia blushed at the thought of seeing Hadrian's

Wall with Roman as her guide, but the pleasure faded quickly as she remembered that he thought she was Garry's mistress. He wouldn't want anything to do with her once they caught up with the missing pair.

He wouldn't like being made a fool of, even it was largely his own fault for refusing to believe her when she told him about Dana. She said goodnight and almost ran into her room, and, contrary to her expectations, slept soundly.

She woke slowly from a vague dream as an errant breeze drifted over her face, coming to rest on her mouth. She murmured in protest as the gentle touch turned into a force that raised emotions she had thought were impossible in any dream. Her eyes flew open as Roman kissed her again, his hands stroking the soft shoulders, revealed by her scanty nightdress.

She struggled to sit up, still wrapped in the mists of sleep, and he transferred his gaze from her shoulders to her breasts. She grabbed the sheet and he laughed.

'Spoil-sport,' he said, his eyes darkening.

'What are you doing in here, and how did you get in?' she asked, her voice by no means as steady as she wished.

'I came to wake you, and I got in through the bathroom, which you forgot to lock.' Claudia glared at him; but he sounded amused, and she drew a breath of relief. Roman in a temper she could do without.

'Up you get,' he said with one of the changes of mood she found so devastating, and she wondered if

that was one of the Sagittarian characteristics Myra
thought she should explore.

'It's ten o'clock; they'll be back from the coach
tour at two and I want to be there to meet them. I'm
not giving Garry a chance to skip off again.'

'There are four hours before they arrive,' Claudia
said quietly. 'I should think that's plenty of time, but
if you were afraid it isn't you could have woken me
earlier.' Roman ran a hand through his hair, a thing
he had done more than once this morning if its state
was anything to go by.

'I'm sorry, I'm on edge, but I shouldn't take it out
on you—you can't be exactly jumping for joy at the
thought of seeing Garry with another woman.'

Claudia shrugged her shoulders; that aspect of it
only bothered her because of the way Dana might
react.

'You're taking this very calmly. I can almost
accept your tale of a carbon-copy twin.'

'I'm telling the truth. Now, if you'll get out of my
room, I'll get dressed.'

'What if I decide to stay and enjoy the floor show?'

'Then I stay here.' She clutched the sheet round
her so tightly that her knuckles turned white.

'Such an enthusiastic invitation! You don't have
to worry; I'm going. I'll give you fifteen minutes.'

'Miser,' Claudia yelled. 'I need thirty.' A chuckle
was her only answer as he closed the door behind
him, and she jumped out of bed and into the
bathroom in case he had been serious about the
fifteen minutes.

'I like a woman who can keep to the time I give
her,' Roman said as she came into their sitting-

room. He looked with appreciation at her deep
cream pleated skirt and cream and jade blouse,
while in her turn Claudia thought how well the tan
trousers and matching shirt suited him, moulding his
large frame lovingly and making his amber eyes
appear gold.

The small table in the window was set for breakfast for one. Roman said he had already eaten but
that he would have another cup of coffee. Under his
critical gaze, Claudia ate scrambled eggs and bacon
instead of her usual slice of toast. He sipped his
coffee and smiled warmly.

'I approve of a woman who doesn't watch every
mouthful,' he said.

'I could get fat,' Claudia teased: she liked the
relaxed atmosphere between them this morning and
hoped it would continue, at least until they met up
with Dana and Garry.

A tight knot of apprehension made her frown and,
as if he knew just what she was thinking, he got to
his feet.

'I'll phone the hotel to check the time of Garry's
arrival,' he said and, picking up the phone, he asked
to be connected with the Crowned Head. A few
minutes later he banged the receiver down and
turned to Claudia, a heavy scowl on his face.

'What's the matter?' she said in alarm. 'Has there
been an accident?' Her heart throbbed heavily at the
thought that Dana could be hurt, perhaps worse.
She jumped up and seized his arm, tears starting to
her eyes.

'You're very concerned for a man who, to put it
bluntly, has ditched you,' he said nastily.

'Answer me, damn you,' Claudia shouted, beside herself with fear for Dana. Roman's mouth hardened into a straight line.

'So he does mean something to you, despite all your denials?' Claudia gave a gasp of protest and he took pity on her obvious distress.

'There hasn't been an accident,' he said tersely.

'No, of course there hasn't, I'd have known if Dana had been hurt in any way. I'm sorry I panicked, but there is something wrong, isn't there?'

'That stupid receptionist didn't tell me there was an optional extra day on that tour—they won't be back until tomorrow.' Claudia leaned against him. For a moment she really had thought Dana had been hurt. Roman caught her before she could fall and carried her to the small settee. It wasn't really large enough for two, but she wasn't about to complain; she needed the comfort of his arms.

'You were really upset, weren't you?' he murmured. 'What will it take before you realise he's just not worth the anguish?'

'I don't care about Garry. How can I when I don't know him? I was afraid Dana had been hurt, though if I'd stopped to think I would have known she wasn't.'

Roman shook his head in weary disgust. 'Not that again. . .you never give up, do you? You're so obsessed with belonging to a twin sign that you've imagined you really have one.'

'Only a double-dealing Sagittarius could think such a thing,' Claudia said indignantly.

'If anyone is double-dealing it's you. This twin of yours is pure fiction, but I do think you know who

Garry's new love is. Continue to play tricks if it amuses you, Claudia—no doubt the truth will be revealed when we meet up with them. In the meantime I suggest we follow their example.'

'What do you mean?' Claudia leapt off the settee and darted to the door, only to stop as she heard him laugh.

'Not what you're thinking,' he said, a wicked twinkle in his eyes. 'You thought I meant we should pass the time in bed, didn't you? No, don't bother to deny it—your blush gives you away.'

Claudia put her hands to her burning face and wished she could fall through the floor. That was exactly what she had thought.

'Relax, Claudia,' he said, his deep voice sending shivers down her spine. 'I meant we should take a trip to Hadrian's wall.'

Claudia lowered her hands and her eyes began to dance. 'Could we? I'd like that,' she said, feeling as if he had given her a priceless gift.

'We could and we will. Pack a case while I inform the hotel that we'll be away overnight.' He lifted the phone and she followed his instructions to such good effect that fifteen minutes later she came back into the sitting-room, her overnight case in her hand.

She knew immediately that Roman's mood had changed; he was looking as grim as when they had first met, but he said nothing as they got into the car.

'Is anything wrong?' she asked anxiously as they left the town behind them. For a few minutes he remained silent and she wondered where the bright start to the day had gone.

'I phoned the hospital and Berenice isn't so well. She's fretting over Garry's absence, and according to her doctor it's important that he gets in touch with her without delay.' He slammed his fist on the steering-wheel. 'I'll kill that bastard when I find him.' He turned amber eyes to her. 'I suppose I shouldn't blame you entirely; you're not with him this time.'

'Wouldn't it be better if we stayed in Alnwick?' Claudia ventured quietly. 'You might want to phone the hospital again.'

'I can phone from anywhere, and I'll go mad if I have nothing to take my mind off that worthless brother-in-law of mine, but I've changed my mind about the wall. We could meet up with them in public and I couldn't guarantee not to strangle him on sight. Berenice is in no immediate danger and I'd prefer to confront Garry in the privacy of his hotel room.' He smiled wryly. 'I'm sorry to disappoint you, but Hadrian and his wall will have to wait for another time.'

Claudia was disappointed, but she also understood. The last thing she wanted was to meet Dana and Garry face to face in a place crowded with tourists.

'Don't let it worry you,' she said. 'I can see the wall another day.' His hands relaxed from their tight grip on the steering-wheel; she must have said the right thing for once.

'Where are we heading now?' she asked in an effort to salvage something from the day if it was at all possible. He laughed, the corners of his eyes crinkling attractively.

'I thought you might like to go to Lindisfarne— Holy Island,' he added as she stared at him blankly. She smiled, her face brightening.

'I should like that very much, but you must have been there many times before.'

'I have, but it's a fascinating place and always casts a fresh spell over me, though this trip the island won't be the only thing to enchant me.'

Claudia felt the colour rise to her face, and he chuckled. Trust him not to miss that. She turned her face to the window and was rewarded by a view of the sea in the distance. The countryside was lovely, and she didn't have to pretend to be absorbed in it.

'Can you tell me about Lin——? What did you call it?' she said as the silence started to grow oppressive.

'Lindisfarne, but Holy Island will do. It was called that when St Aidan established a monastery there. It has long since disappeared, ravaged by Vikings, but the ruins of the Norman priory are still there, and very lovely they are. There is also a castle that's worth a visit.' He sounded friendly, his grim mood lifting as he concentrated on his driving and the island they were going to visit.

They stopped for lunch in Bamburgh, where their table in the small restaurant had a view of the castle set on a crag above the village.

'Bamburgh Castle,' Roman said in answer to her look of enquiry. 'Home for the kings of Northumberland and the first English castle ever to

be damaged by gunfire. It's completely restored and
it was used for several films—*Macbeth* and *Becket*,
to name two of them. We haven't time to visit it
now—we'll miss the tide if we delay much longer.'

He hurried her out of the restaurant and she took
a last look at the castle as he drove past, promising
herself she would return one day.

'Don't look so wistful—there will be another time
for Bamburgh,' he said quietly, and she wondered
why he was talking as if they had a future together.
He was only being polite, saying the things you did
say to someone to whom you were close in an
unusual situation.

Once he had Garry back with Berenice he
wouldn't give a thought to the Adams twins and she
would forget him and the time she had spent hunting
Garry and her sister through the Northumberland
countryside.

Claudia pleated her skirt between her fingers.
Roman would forget her but she doubted that she
would be so lucky. This dynamic man had entered
her life with an explosive force, and he had damaged
her secure little world, altering it so drastically that
she would never be the same Claudia who had
happily spent her days and most of her evenings
designing dresses for other girls to wear.

She hadn't envied those girls until now; she stole
a look at Roman and admitted to herself that she
was more than attracted to him. She didn't love
him—that would be ridiculous on such a short
dramatic acquaintance. No; it was the romance of
the whole thing that was getting to her; after all, it
wasn't every day you were whisked away on a white

charger. . .well, a modern car made a good substitute. Her lips curved in amusement and Roman asked if he could share the joke. She laughed and, telling him her thoughts were private, settled down to enjoy the rest of the journey.

CHAPTER SIX

LINDISFARNE was a completely new experience for
Claudia. Roman drove steadily over the causeway
and she looked apprehensively at the expanse of sea
on either side.

'Relax,' he said, laughing at her expression.
'We're well clear of the tide and we'll be back on the
mainland before the next one is due.' Claudia
laughed at her own fears; she was quite safe with
Roman—from the sea, anyway. She wasn't so sure
about her safety when it came to other things.

She looked ahead to the island with anticipation.
She and her father had visited many places of
historical interest, including several castles, but the
small castle perched on its rock promised to be
special.

'It's the only castle I've ever seen that I can
imagine living in,' she said, standing in the upper
gallery and gazing at the magnificent views from the
windows.

'Perhaps that's because it was a private home until
its owner gave it to the National Trust. He remained
as tenant, as did his sister after him until she died in
the late sixties.'

'You can tell,' Claudia said simply. 'Most old
castles are too large to be lived in now—you'd need
hordes of retainers.' She laughed up at him and his
eyes gleamed, his gaze fixed on her mouth.

'You'd make a very worthy chatelaine for any man's home,' he murmured, his eyes twinkling with amusement as the colour flooded her face. He took her arm as they strolled away from the castle. The path was stony; that was why she let him hold on to her, and for no other reason.

'How many men had you discarded before you decided to throw your lot in with a married man?' he murmured, so casually that she said,

'None,' before she realised what he had said. She pulled free of him, stopping dead in the middle of the path, causing considerable confusion to people walking towards the castle.

'How dare you ask such a thing?' she hissed. Roman took her arm in a grip she couldn't break and marched her down the path.

'It's a valid question.'

'As you see it,' Claudia jeered. 'Well, this time you're wrong.'

'So you still deny you've been sleeping with Garry?'

'I do. My sister and I may share the same birthday, but we don't share the same man, though if we did it would be none of your business.'

'When it concerns my sister's health it is my business.' He sounded so fiercely protective that she wondered sadly what it would be like to have a man care for her as much as Roman cared for Berenice.

Her father had loved her, but her mother had come first, as was only right, and, under her seeming indifference, her mother had loved and relied on her husband. That was why, Claudia saw suddenly,

Fleur had clung more than ever to Dana after their father's death.

She stumbled on the rough surface and Roman slid his arm round her waist, holding her against him. She was very conscious of the spicy scent from his skin, and a tremor ran through her.

'Are you cold?' he asked, answering his own question immediately. 'No, you can't be. Can I hope your shiver means you're aware of me and what I have in mind for our entertainment tonight?'

Claudia stared blindly at the ground, willing herself not to blush, but unwanted heat swept over her.

'Well, well, so I was right,' he murmured.

'No, you were not; just keep your innuendoes to yourself, at least in public.' She could have kicked herself as she added the last bit.

'Does that mean I'm free to tell you what I think and want when we are alone?' He was openly laughing at her, and she wished she could push him into the sea. At that moment they reached the ruined abbey and she fell silent at its sheer beauty. Outlined against the sky, it was majestic.

'It's awe-inspiring, even after all these years. . .it's poetry translated into stone,' she whispered, and Roman kissed her cheek, oblivious to the other holiday-makers.

'You're very sensitive to atmosphere, aren't you?' He sounded surprised, and Claudia reacted sharply.

'I may spend my days in a welter of silks and satins, but I'm not an entire moron, you know.' Roman took a quick glance at her heavy frown and kissed her again.

'I'm sorry, Claudia. I was out of order, but the

Claudia Adams who enticed Garry away from his wife and the girl I am beginning to know could be two different people.'

Claudia wanted to laugh out loud—that was what she had been telling him for days, but under the joy she was aware of fear making itself known. Fear for Dana and what would happen to her twin if Roman found her and Garry before she could warn her. She met his eyes and as calmly as she could told him she and her father had loved visiting castles and mansions on their holidays.

'Doesn't sound much like a top model—neither does the way you work at your business,' Roman said heavily.

'Perhaps I'm hoping to meet a man rich enough to keep me in comfort so I can indulge my every whim and fancy and give up work for good,' she said drily.

'Is that what you want?'

'Why not?' she said lightly. He moved away, ostensibly to examine a corner of the abbey, but she saw his eyes were colder than the stones of which it was built. Her heart sank; she had been so intent on trying to score off him that she hadn't given a thought to what her careless words could do to the understanding that had seemed to be developing between them.

She stroked a sun-warmed block of stone with fingers that trembled. She wanted to tell him that she hadn't meant a word she had said, but if she did he would think she was hoping he was the rich man she had talked about.

She cursed her errant tongue, but she was so frustrated and pained by his persistence in thinking she was the author of Berenice's present troubles that she had rushed into speech, with dire consequences.

She straightened her shoulders and gazed up at the unremitting blue of the sky. A solitary seagull winged its way over the sea; it looked as lonely as she felt.

It was no use deceiving herself any longer. She loved Roman with all her heart and soul, and she doubted if she would be able to even look at another man for the rest of her life.

A sob, swiftly repressed, rose in her throat; she was condemning herself to a life as lonely as the seagull's looked, but it, at least, could find a mate— she would never be able to do that. She looked at Roman, so strong and dependable; any woman would give thanks every day of her life for a man like him, and she had just ruined any chance she had of being that woman. She lifted a hand to her head; it was aching badly. Roman abandoned his examination of the wall that had seemed to fascinate him, and came over to her.

'Aren't you feeling well, Claudia? You're very pale.'

'I have a headache—too much sun, I expect. It'll go.'

'We'll go back to the car. You've had enough for one day.' He walked by her side without touching her, even when she tripped on the uneven turf, and she knew she had destroyed anything there might have been.

It was better this way; somehow she would manage to see Dana before Roman did, and then she would leave and take up her life as it had been before she had met Roman almost a week ago.

Five short days; it wasn't long in which to have your life turned upside-down, changed so drastically that it would never be the same again, was it? But it had happened, and there was nothing she could do about it.

They drove back to Alnwick in complete silence, broken only as they reached their suite, by Roman.

'Dinner in half an hour—be ready,' he said curtly as his door closed behind him with a decisive click. Claudia sank down on to her bed and tried to shut her ears to the sound of him in the next room.

It proved impossible; her senses were heightened to such a degree that she could hear every move he made. She took herself off to the bathroom, carefully locking both doors before shedding her clothes. She stood under the shower and told herself it was the water that was running down her face and not tears. Why should she cry? She would soon be free to go her own way once more, and that was what she wanted, wasn't it?

She was ready and waiting when Roman tapped on her door. He was dressed in the silver-grey trousers of the evening before, teamed with a cream shirt, and she wrenched her gaze away from his strong throat, revealed by the open neck, with an effort.

It was getting harder every minute she spent with him to pretend an indifference she didn't feel, but she must never let him know how much she loved him.

He glanced over her slowly from head to foot,

taking in the sleeveless green cotton dress with its tight bodice and full skirt that had seemed so modest when she had put it on. It didn't seem modest now; it could have been transparent, from the way his amber eyes lingered on every inch of the body he was mentally stripping.

'Blushing again? You should patent your secret— it would fetch a fortune from would-be innocents out to snare a man.' He held the door open for her and she was very careful not to touch him as she passed. He looked as if he would like to sear her with another acid remark but he remained silent, as she did, apart from a few non-committal remarks, all through dinner.

Claudia couldn't eat more than a morsel of the beef Roman had ordered. She managed the ice-cream dessert a bit better—it required little effort to swallow—though she couldn't taste a thing.

'I'm going for a walk,' Roman said abruptly as they left the dining-room, and without waiting for a reply he left her standing by the lifts.

'Just like a wet lettuce waiting for a plate,' she muttered, colouring at the strange looks she received. Suddenly she swung round on her heels and left the hotel. She couldn't stand the thought of being shut in her room waiting for Roman to return. Not that he would come to her—his manner ever since her remarks about finding a rich man had indicated quite clearly that the sooner they could part company, the better it would suit him.

Alnwick had a relaxed air this evening that was a complete contrast to the bustle that prevailed during the day. Couples of all ages strolled leisurely along, stopping now and then to look in shop windows.

Claudia paused at one, attracted by a display of unusual ornaments made of mother-of-pear. They were beautiful, and she would have loved to be able to buy one, but even the simplest was far beyond her pocket. Dreams was doing well but luxuries like these were still in the distant future.

'Dreaming of weddings and the rings that go with them?' The deep sardonic voice made her gasp. Roman had come up behind her without warning, and she had been so engrossed with the window display that her senses, which usually warned her if he was near, had failed.

'Rings?' she said, puzzled by his words.

'Wedding-rings and engagement rings. . .the ones you were gazing at so rapturously.' He gestured to the window and Claudia saw that a display of rings was next to the ornaments she admired.

With resignation she felt the colour steal into her face, and knew he wouldn't believe her even as she tried to explain that she hadn't even seen the rings but had been absorbed by the ornaments. His raised eyebrows confirmed her fears, and she was surprised when he looked closely at the display.

'Which one do you like?' he asked, and she laughed in relief at his normal tone. Her companion of the earlier part of the day seemed to have returned.

'I like them all, but liking is as far as I'll get— have you seen the prices?'

'They're not exorbitant for craftsmanship of that quality,' he said, bending his head for a closer look at an exquisite rose fashioned from mother-of-pearl and spun gold. One petal held a beautiful, almost translucent pear-shaped dewdrop and it was set in a crystal vase that looked as substantial as a spider's web.

'That one,' Claudia breathed. She glanced at the discreet price tag and laughed. 'Trust me to pick the most expensive.'

'Might as well go for the best,' Roman said, and Claudia wrinkled her nose at him.

'Not with my income, even if roses are my flower, but I do think it's lovely. The artist must have been inspired, and pearls are my birthstone.'

'Not that again,' he groaned, 'but do you really prefer the rose to diamonds? It isn't as valuable by a long way.'

'That's a funny question. You can hardly compare a mother-of-pearl flower to a diamond ring. They're both lovely in their own way.' Roman nodded as if she had confirmed his thoughts, and turned away from the window, taking her with him.

Claudia thought of resisting, but one look at his grim expression told her it would be useless. What had she said to make him look like that? They walked back to the hotel in a silence that was becoming unhappily familiar.

He followed her into the lift and she counted the floors, wanting only to close her bedroom door behind her. Roman was by her side as she inserted her key in the lock. She said goodnight over her shoulder and tried to shut the door, but he was so near that it was impossible. He closed and locked the door and she felt crowded, even though the room was by no means small.

'I think it's time we got things straight between us,' he said grimly.

Claudia shook her head in bewilderment.

'You must have thought me very slow not to get your meaning days ago.'

'What meaning? You're talking like a crossword puzzle, and I'm no good at puzzles.'

'I think you know exactly what I mean, but if it makes you happy I'll spell it out. I want you, but I have no intention of giving you a plain gold ring or any other ring that could be held against me as a pledge. I'll be generous in other ways—I'll even put my intentions in writing if that will help persuade you of my sincerity. Yes, that would be best. You have no reason to trust me, and I trust no woman except my sister.

'Well, is it a deal?' He held his hand out, but Claudia kept hers tightly clenched at her side. He was so strong and confident, so sure of himself, that it was a pity he held all women in contempt. Berenice, lucky Berenice, was the one exception.

'Well?' he said again, and she looked at him, anger taking over from the sadness his offer had brought.

'My answer is no; there will be no deal of any kind between us. I'm here because you forced me to come, and I'll leave as soon as you find your brother-in-law.'

'Is that your last word? I'm sure I could persuade you to reconsider.'

Claudia stepped back hastily, her hands held out in front of her. 'I won't change my mind.'

'Are you certain? You don't sound it.' He moved quickly, pulling her forcefully into his arms. His mouth was hard and hot, burning her lips with an intensity of desire that brought an involuntary response. The kiss went on forever, and she offered no resistance as he swung her up into his arms and dropped her gently on the bed, coming down with her.

If it hadn't been for the triumphant glitter in his eyes she would have been lost; as it was, he had pulled her zip down and was easing her dress from her shoulders by the time she'd steeled herself to thrust hard against his shoulders with both hands and roll off the bed.

She clutched her dress to her and looked at him with as much scorn as she could.

'I meant what I said, and you can't change my mind by caveman tactics.'

'Is that what they are? I must be slipping,' he said, a hint of laughter in his voice. He was still lying on her bed, his head propped up on one hand. He looked like a tiger baulked of its prey, but the amusement was only on the surface; underneath he was furious that she should dare to try to escape him.

She moistened her lips with the tip of her tongue and his sudden tension told her she was right. Roman didn't take kindly to any woman's refusal, and he no doubt thought he was doing her an honour in wanting her when he thought she had belonged to

Garry. He got off the bed, uncoiling to his full height, and she felt threatened as never before.

'I won't take your refusal,' he said in a soft voice that made her quake. 'You'll do as I wish sooner or later.'

'No,' she said, looking him straight in the eye and immediately wishing she hadn't. 'I won't be your mistress.'

'Why not? You were Garry's—why not turn to me?'

'Perhaps once was enough,' she said before she could stop.

'I can be much more generous than Garry.'

'I could be looking for something more,' she said, and again she wished she had kept her mouth closed, but he seemed to bring out the worse in her, and she couldn't resist answering his insults in the only way she knew. She wanted him to believe the truth about her, but he never would; someone had destroyed his trust in women and she wasn't the one to restore it.

Even when he knew she was speaking the truth about Dana he would continue to think she was out for all she could get, and she had only herself to blame.

'You're holding out for a wedding-ring,' he said flatly. 'That is the one thing I will never offer any woman again.' He scowled heavily; obviously he regretted saying so much.

'Again? So you did want to get married once?'

'Once, when I was young and stupid, but I've always been thankful my intended bride broke our engagement when she found a wealthier man than the young fool who was working flat out to save the

almost bankrupt business his father had left him.'
His voice dropped to a seductive murmur.

'We could be happy together, once you come to
terms with the fact that marriage isn't on my
agenda.'

'It's on mine,' Claudia said bleakly. 'So I must
decline your offer. You've had a bad experience,
but it's one that happens to both men and women
and you should have forgotten it long ago. You must
know by now that women are not all the same.'

He smiled, a slow cynical twist of his lips that left
his eyes empty of all emotion.

'My personal knowledge tells me differently.
Sooner or later a woman will show her true nature.
I wouldn't trust even the most loving one not to
leave when another man offers more.' He held out
his hand. 'I don't see why you can't come to me until
your dream man comes along,' he said, and she
wanted to hit him, all the sympathy she had felt
drowning in his sarcasm. Her silence spoke for her
and he turned to his room, anger making his eyes
glitter.

'If you change your mind, you know where I am.'
The quiet click of the latch sounded like a death-
knell in the silent room, and she sank down on the
bed, her mind and heart devoid of hope.

Not surprisingly she passed a less than restful
night, only falling asleep as the light started to
penetrate the thin curtains, and when she did finally
surface the sun was high in the sky and her room
was like an oven.

The threw back the bedclothes, shed her clinging
nightgown and stood under a cool shower until she

began to come alive. Half an hour later, dressed in
a yellow sundress sprinkled with white daisies, held
up by narrow straps with a wide sash for a belt, she
looked as cool as she felt. She hadn't heard a sound
from Roman's room and she hoped he was out.

She glanced at her watch, realising she didn't
know when Dana and Garry were due back. She
would have to make enquiries at once. Panic at the
thought of Roman's meeting Dana without her sent
her hurrying to the reception and its public phone.

'I've already phoned,' Roman said as she lifted
the receiver. Claudia looked at him with resignation;
of course he had. . .he'd never let a trick pass him
by. She cloaked her embarrassment at seeing him by
rushing into speech.

'When are they due back, do you know?'

'Keen to see Garry again. Aren't you worried
about meeting his new girlfriend?' She shot him a
look designed to kill at fifty feet, but he only raised
one eyebrow in mute enquiry.

'I only want this farce to be over so I can get on
with my life.'

'Without me, you mean? I'm not at all sure I shall
allow that,' he said smoothly. Claudia swung away.
She was blushing again, with anger, she assured
herself. A hand on her arm stopped her before she
had taken more than three steps.

'In answer to your question, the coach is due in an
hour—plenty of time for you to have breakfast.'

'How do you know I haven't already eaten?' she
asked. A slow smile curved his well-shaped mouth.

'You haven't had time. I looked in on you a short
while ago and you were fast asleep. I nearly joined

you, but when we do make love we'll have all the
time in the world, not just a few snatched minutes.'

Claudia was getting used to feeling like a red rose
in full bloom but it didn't make her like the feeling,
or the man whose remarks caused her discomfort.
She followed him into the dining-room and sat
quietly while he ordered breakfast for her. Roman
drank coffee while she ate as quickly as she could.

'I've also phoned the hospital,' he said at one
point.

'How's your sister?' Claudia asked, afraid he
would say Berenice was worse. He banged his cup
down on its saucer, so hard that she expected it to
shatter.

'Much the same. . .missing Garry badly while
trying to put up a brave pretence of not interfering
with his work. You can imagine how that makes me
feel,' he said bitterly. 'I'm supposedly responsible
for keeping him away.' He stirred the dregs of his
coffee with a brooding intensity she could feel all
through her.

It was imperative that she should reach Dana
before he did. She would tell her twin about
Berenice's baby, and if she knew her sister, she
would make Garry see he must return to his wife.
She finished eating, hoping she could elude Roman
and get to Dana's hotel without him, but as soon as
she put her cup down he was urging her to her feet.

'I want to be there before the coach gets in,' he
said urgently. She went with him, her heart beating
heavily. He was so angry that she feared for both
Dana and Garry. Garry deserved all that was coming
to him; fidelity in marriage seemed to be very little

regarded but Garry must have known about the
baby and there was no excuse for him.

Roman settled them at one of the small tables in
a garden at the side of the yard at the Crowned
Head. He summoned a girl, who seemed mesmer-
ised by his virile look, and ordered lager for them
both.

'I need something stronger than coffee,' he said,
and Claudia could see that he was under considerable strain. Ten minutes later a large green and
white coach slid into view, coming to rest in the
middle of the yard.

Roman tugged Claudia to her feet and rushed her
out of the garden before the coach doors had time
to open. Silently they watched the passengers leave,
and only when the last ones had laughed and chatted
their way into the hotel did Claudia manage to
relax.

'They weren't on it,' Roman said incredulously,
and she realised that, though she had been thankful
not to see Dana, Roman must be worried sick about
Berenice and livid that Garry had, once again,
escaped him.

Her brows puckered in a frown, she gazed at the
deserted coach, and she didn't realise that Roman
had left her until he returned, a furious expression
on his face.

'Several of the passengers left the coach near the
shopping centre,' he said harshly.

'They'll come back soon,' Claudia said quietly. He
looked at her as if she were an idiot.

'I'm aware of that, but I can't sit here and await
their pleasure. This isn't a very large town; I'm going

to look for them. You can come or not, as you please.'

'I'll wait here,' Claudia said with no intention of doing anything of the kind.

'Fine,' he said and strode across the yard, his shoes ringing sharply on the cobbles. Claudia waited until he reached the street before leaving the yard herself.

CHAPTER SEVEN

CLAUDIA was careful to keep several people between her and Roman. It wouldn't do for him to look round and see her; on the other hand, she wanted to reach the shops before he did.

She had one advantage over him; he had only a general idea of which shops would interest Garry and his 'Mrs Smith', but Claudia knew Dana would make straight for the most exclusive dress shops, and luckily Claudia had a very good idea which one would be at the top of her list.

She stopped briefly, pulled her sash free and put it over her head, tucking her hair under it. Roman would be less likely to spot her now if he chanced to look round.

She dived down a narrow lane, and within minutes she was in front of a small shop with the name 'Suzanne' in gilt letters over the bow-windows. Yesterday there had only been one dress on display. A scintillating mixture of blues and greens, it was just the kind of thing Dana would love.

It had gone now, its place taken by a summer suit Claudia loved at first sight, but she wasn't here to buy clothes—she must find Dana. She hesitated. It had seemed a good idea, but how could she ask for Dana in a strange shop? She peered through the glass door, half inclined to look for Dana in the bigger stores, when she was riveted by the sight of her twin appearing from behind a curtain.

She was wearing the blue and green dress and it suited her every bit as well Claudia had thought it would. She watched as Dana twirled and twisted before a long mirror, making the dress shimmer with a thousand lights.

Claudia decided to wait outside. Dana would be startled to see her, and a scene was the last thing either of them needed. At that moment Dana raised her head and looked straight at Claudia. Her eyes widened and for a moment she looked scared, but her model's training stood her in good stead and she showed no other sign of what must have been a shock.

She turned abruptly into the fitting-room and after a very short time reappeared, looking as perfect as if she had spent hours dressing instead of minutes. She spoke to the sales girl, and Claudia, thinking she was buying the dress, looked longingly at the smoky-blue suit she coveted, and she didn't notice the door open until a hand on her arm brought her attention to her twin.

Dana was angry. Claudia saw the unmistakable signs with dismay.

'How did you find me? What right have you to follow me here?' Dana demanded, her voice shrill with rage.

'It's a long story and one I can't tell you in the street. Can we find a café or somewhere? It's not a good idea to stand in plain sight.' She saw a small coffee shop on the other side of the lane and, taking Dana's arm, tried to pull her with her.

'I'm going nowhere until you tell me why you're here.'

'Please, Dana, do as I ask; it's important,' Claudia pleaded, and something in her manner must have got across, for after a few seconds Dana allowed herself to be led towards the café.

'I don't know what this is all about, or why you're acting as if the bogyman is on your heels, but I suppose I'll have to listen to you.' Dana cast Claudia a disparaging glance. 'That scarf thing does nothing for you, sister, dear,' she said mockingly. She tweaked the pale blue hat she was wearing with a look of satisfaction and walked into the café to a table in a corner.

'What are you doing here?' Dana said as soon as the waitress had brought their tea. 'How did you know we'd be in Alnwick? I told no one, so how did you find us?' Claudia noted the plural with a sinking feeling; she had known Dana was with Garry, but some part of her had denied that knowledge.

'I didn't find you—Roman did,' she said simply, seeing Dana's colour fade at the mention of Roman's name.

'How do you come to know Roman Wyatt?' Dana spat. 'I suppose you went running to him after my phone call.'

'How could I? I didn't know his name, or even Garry's surname. He found me. He's had you watched. Garry's wife suspected there was another woman and she was so upset that she turned to her brother for help.'

'Just like that feeble Berenice,' Dana said, her lip curling with disdain. 'She can't keep her husband

and won't let anyone else have him. The woman has
no pride.'

'That may be true,' Claudia said, knowing that
were she in Berenice's shoes, she would let Garry
go. Would she, though, if the man were Roman?
She closed her eyes as pain lanced through her. She
wasn't going to be given the chance. Roman would
gladly say goodbye now he was about to catch up
with Garry.

'What does Roman Wyatt want?' Dana said
urgently, and Claudia wrenched her attention back
to her twin.

'Do you need to ask? He wants Garry to go back
to Berenice, and it's important he does go, at once.'

'Fat chance of that,' Dana sneered. 'Garry has
finished with her. He has independent means, and
we're going to enjoy every minute of our lives
together.'

Claudia felt a deep pang of sorrow for her sister.
Dana sounded very confident, but she didn't know
about the baby. She leaned forward and placed her
hand on Dana's.

'It's not quite as easy as that,' she said, her voice
so full of sympathy that Dana looked up in alarm.

'What is it? I can tell something is wrong and that
you're dying to spoil things for me. I know you've
always been jealous of my success as a model, but I
won't allow you to ruin things for Garry and me.'
She wrenched her hand away from Claudia's and got
to her feet.

'I'm leaving. You can keep your reason for hunting me down to yourself.' Claudia pulled her wits
together. The shock of hearing Dana say she was

jealous would have to be pushed to the back of her mind for now. Dana mustn't leave without hearing about Berenice.

'Sit down, Dana,' she said, with such authority that, to both their astonishment, she instantly obeyed.

'Well?' she said sulkily. 'Tell me this earth-shattering news of yours.'

'It has nothing to do with me personally,' Claudia said calmly.

'It's Berenice; she's going to have a baby.'

'Is that all? There's nothing new in that—she's been trying for years. Garry went along with her to divert suspicion from us.'

'You didn't care that Garry was still sleeping with his wife when he was supposed to be in love with you?' Claudia wondered if she had ever known Dana. In her place she couldn't have stood that for one moment, but neither could she take a man from his wife.

'You're too good to be true,' Dana said. 'It's time you learnt to look after yourself, or else you'll find you're firmly on an unreachable shelf. If Berenice manages to have a child that will let Garry off the hook.'

'Perhaps it could, but she's in trouble. If Garry doesn't appear soon she could well lose it, and if she does her health could be endangered.'

Dana stirred her tea, swirling it round and round so rapidly that Claudia thought she would wash it out of the cup.

She raised troubled eyes to her sister, and for the first time Claudia saw a glimpse of the Dana she had

been before ambition and the love of money had
taken over her life.

'I don't want to hurt Berenice. I didn't know
about the baby.' Her lips trembled and Claudia put
a hand on hers, grasping it firmly.

'I know you didn't, but, now that you do, what
will you do?'

'I don't know, I really don't. I've been so happy
since I met Garry. You've always been so strong
that you don't know what it's been like for me since
mother died.'

'You've always had me,' Claudia said quietly.
How little Dana knew her; the strength she admired
was mostly window-dressing. Underneath she was as
uncertain as her twin. Dana dabbed her eyes with a
fine lace handkerchief, careful not to smudge her
eye make-up, Claudia noted with indulgence.

'You're my sister, it's true, but I need a man I can
rely on,' Dana said, regaining her confidence
rapidly.

'And Garry is that man?'

'I thought he was; now I'm not so sure. He could
go back to his wife, though why he should I don't
really know. She won't want for money—her
wealthy brother will see to that. What more can she
expect or want?'

'She can expect her husband at her side, and that's
what she's going to get.' The harsh voice made both
women jump, and Claudia felt the blood drain from
her face. Roman; what was he doing here. . .how
had he found them?

'I knew you were following me as soon as you left
the hotel yard, and I decided to turn the tables. It

wasn't difficult; I lost you for a moment when you covered your hair, but I know you too well for you to be able to hide from me.'

Both Dana and Claudia were standing now, and Claudia knew Dana was weighing up her chance of escape.

Don't try it, she said silently, knowing Dana had received the message by the way her eyes widened.

'So you were telling the truth,' Roman said, his eyes going from one to the other. 'I wouldn't have believed two people could be so exactly alike; you are, of course, identical twins.'

'Unfortunately, yes,' Dana hissed. 'If it hadn't been for that you'd never have found us.'

'I wouldn't count on that,' Roman said almost lazily, but there was nothing languid in the glance he gave Claudia. 'I'd have found Garry sooner or later, but I still don't know why my detective didn't know there were two of you.'

'Perhaps this will explain,' Dana whipped off her hat and laughed at the look on their faces.

'You've changed your hair colour,' Claudia said, gazing at the blonde curls that fell round Dana's shoulders.

'Marvellous, isn't it? You should try it sometimes, sister, dear, instead of the boring brown-mouse colour you cling to.'

'This is a recent change, I take it?' Roman said, his eyes on Dana.

'It is—I just wish I'd thought of it years ago.' She laughed again and Claudia was glad her attention was on Roman and she didn't see how upset her twin was by her remarks. Why had she never realised before now that Dana resented looking like her sister?

'I expect Claudia has told you about Berenice,' Roman said, sharply cutting across Dana's self-satisfaction. Dana nodded sulkily and Claudia could have slapped her; this wasn't the time for Dana to hold centre stage. 'Then you know that time is of the utmost importance?' he continued. Dana shrugged her shoulders.

'Berenice is nothing to do with Garry any more. We've cut all ties with our old lives and we're going to be together from now on,' she said defiantly. Roman looked at her in a way that made Claudia want to curl up and die, and she wasn't on the receiving end, only tarred with the same brush. If he had ever had any feeling for her it was now stone-dead.

'I want to hear that from Garry, and I intend to see him, with or without your co-operation.' He turned eyes hard with disgust on Dana, and Claudia wasn't at all surprised when her sister mumbled that Garry was waiting for her in a café in the main street.

'Right, we'll go there now.' He ushered both girls out of the building and, putting his arm round Claudia, took Dana's arm in a firm grip.

'We can't walk three abreast,' Claudia said as they emerged into the lane filled with people. Roman's lips curled slightly; he started to walk and the stream of people automatically flowed apart as they approached, leaving them a clear path.

Just as the Red Sea parted for the Israelites, Claudia thought, not at all surprised at their easy passage. She could have wished it otherwise—then she might have been able to lose herself in the crowd. She had no desire to be with Dana and Roman when they met Garry.

She had a burning desire to pack her case and leave on the first mode of transport she could find— she would even settle for a donkey if there was one. Roman's arm tightened round her waist as if he knew her thoughts, and she gave up all hope of escape, for the moment.

Dana came to stop in front of a large café.

'Garry's waiting in the garden,' she said sullenly. Roman marched them through the café and out through a door leading to a patch of lawn. It was deserted except for one man lounging in a comfortable chair under the shade of a tree, an empty glass on a table at his side.

His eyes were closed and he looked completely at ease. Roman, his mouth set in a straight line, strode across the grass, leaving Dana and Claudia to follow. Claudia thought briefly about leaving but Dana sent her a look of such mute appeal that she sighed and followed her twin.

Roman placed a large hand on Garry's shoulder and shook him awake. He jumped up in alarm. He was shorter than Roman, sandy-haired, with pale blue eyes, and to Claudia's mind fell short of Roman in every way. She turned puzzled eyes to Dana. What could her twin see in this very ordinary-looking male? Dana scowled and Claudia knew she had picked up her thoughts.

'Roman; what are you doing here?' Garry sounded frightened, and the look he gave Dana was full of apprehension. He also looked amazed when he saw Claudia.

'I've come to take you back to London,' Roman said. 'This is Claudia, Dana's twin sister.' Garry smiled weakly before turning back to Roman.

'You've wasted your time, Roman,' he said with more resolution than Claudia would have believed possible. 'Berenice and I are finished. My life lies with Dana now. We're going abroad, so Berenice will be able to get a divorce easily.'

'For desertion?' Roman asked mildly, and Garry's rather weak features took on a look of self-congratulation. Claudia could have warned him to beware of Roman when that note entered his voice but Dana and Garry were smiling at each other in mutual satisfaction.

'Are you also happy at deserting your unborn child?' Roman enquired, so quietly that it took a moment before his meaning sank in. Garry went white and Dana looked furious. She opened her mouth to speak, but Garry spoke first.

'Are you trying to tell me Berenice is pregnant, because if you are I don't believe you. I would have been the first to know.'

'So you would, *if* you'd been at home,' Roman rapped, his quietness discarded for an anger that made Claudia shiver. Garry sat down heavily, and Claudia could almost feel sorry for him.

'I haven't been absent all that long,' he protested. 'She must known for some time.'

'She has, but she wanted to make sure it would be all right before telling you. She didn't want to disappoint you again,' he added savagely. Garry gulped visibly.

'Are you saying she isn't all right?' he said hoarsely.

'It's in the balance at the moment. Berenice's blood-pressure is far too high and the doctors are insistent she mustn't have worries of any kind if she's to go to full term.' Roman paused and looked Garry straight in the eyes, holding him captive with an implacable amber gaze.

'I think you know how serious it could be if she lost this child. I have, so far, managed to cover for you, but your wife needs you very badly and my excuses won't hold up much longer.'

'There are reasons why I can't go back, apart from. . .' Garry didn't finish the sentence, but his look at Dana was eloquent enough.

'The orders that have gone astray and the accounts that are far from perfect?' Roman said, his deep voice cynical. 'I've also covered those for you—so far.' Garry's shrug spoke volumes, as did the way he turned away from Dana and started to walk across the lawn. Dana ran after him, catching his arm and bringing him to a standstill.

'You can't do this to us, Garry, you just can't,' she screamed. Garry looked tired of the whole thing, Dana included.

'I have no choice. If I don't go along with Roman I could well land in gaol, and I wouldn't be any good to anyone behind bars, would I? Then there's Berenice and the child. Despite what you all must think, I do care for Berenice, and I'll look after her and our child.' He shook off Dana's hand and walked heavily away. Dana stared after him for a moment, then turned a malevolent glare on Claudia.

'I blame you for this. . . I'll never forgive you, never.' She hurried after Garry, and Roman strode after her, leaving Claudia standing in the middle of the garden feeling as if her world had fallen to pieces round her. The scent of roses wafted to her, carried by an errant breeze, and she sighed. Roses were a Gemini flower and she loved them, but at this moment their beauty meant nothing. It hadn't taken Roman long to transfer his attention to Dana, had it? He had forgotten her in his efforts to catch up with her twin.

Claudia walked slowly back to the hotel; she could leave Alnwick now before Roman came back, if he did come back. He had been attracted to her, but Dana was so much livelier, her beauty so vivid and she would need consoling.

It shouldn't have taken her long to pack and change out of her sundress into a skirt and blouse, but she found she was folding each garment at least twice, and several times she stood looking out of the window at the busy yard below. She could just see Roman's car and she was blinded by a rush of tears as she realised she would never again sit in it by his side.

She turned away from the window, closed her case, caught up her jacket and bag and walked to the door. It was flung open, and she side-stepped hastily, only just avoiding being knocked down by a very annoyed Roman.

He took in her formal outfit and the case in her hand with one sharp glance. He pushed her back into the room and, seizing the case, opened it and upended it over the bed.

'Going somewhere, were you?' he said placidly, but Claudia, looking beyond his tone to the deep glitter in his eyes, couldn't answer. When she could she lifted her head, flinging her hair over her shoulders in a gleaming golden-brown mane.

'You don't need me any longer—you've found Garry, and I'm sure he's going to do just as you want, isn't he?'

'If you mean is he going back to his wife, the answer is yes. I don't think he was quite so committed to your sister as she wanted us to believe, and, talking of that lady, how dare you leave me to cope with an hysterical female on my own?' He sounded so hard done-by that Claudia wanted to giggle, a feeling she sternly repressed. Give in to it and he could be coping with another hysterical female.

'I'm sure you're quite capable of dealing with any woman, hysterical or not, and I didn't leave *you*. It was the other way round.'

'Jealous, were you?' he asked softly, and Claudia could have screamed as heat rose to her face. He laughed and pulled her close to him.

'I thought you were following me, Gemini girl,' he said huskily. 'It took some time to bring your sister to a reasonable state of mind and to prevent her following Garry back to London. I needed your help, Claudia, and when I realised you'd disappeared I knew you'd try to leave without seeing me again. I dumped Dana in the hotel here and rushed to stop you.'

'Why?' Claudia asked. 'Why bring Dana here? She won't want to be near me.'

'I didn't give her a choice. I wanted to give Garry a chance to get clear.' He glanced at his watch. 'He should be leaving about now, and if I know him he'll have left me to pay his hotel bill.

'I don't want your sister running after Garry—she doesn't appear to have much money, so it seemed best to keep her under my eye.' It would have surprised Claudia if Dana did have any money; she earned a great deal but spent it as fast as she made it, and, while it made sense for Roman to bring her under his wing, Claudia resented it fiercely. She leaned against his shoulder, shaken that she should be jealous of her own twin.

'I've turned her loose in the hotel boutique,' Roman murmured, 'so she won't want either of us for some time.'

Surprise that he should know her sister so well, so soon made Claudia lift her head. The amber eyes looked deeply into her's and she was drowning, out of her emotional depth, before she could draw another breath.

'Forget everything except here and now,' Roman said, his deep voice husky with passion. Claudia lifted her arms, putting them round his broad shoulders, hardly conscious that he was divesting her of her jacket and blouse.

She felt her skirt slide over her hips on its way to the floor, and his fingers closed over her breasts as her bra and briefs joined the rest of her clothes. He held her from him and she knew she was blushing all over.

'You're so perfect. . .you even colour like a rose every time I look at you.' He picked her up and lowered her gently on to the bed, shrugging out of his jacket and trousers before joining her.

Claudia tugged at his shirt, sending buttons flying in her impatience to touch his magnificent body. He laughed softly, and soon his strong body and long legs were pressed against her. Never had anyone felt as she did. Claudia closed her eyes and gave herself up to sheer sensation.

She loved everything about this man, and when he took her she tried to stifle the cry of pain. Roman kissed her deeply, murmuring comfortingly before taking them both to heights that owed more to heaven than to earth.

Claudia drifted back slowly to see Roman watching her with a closed expression that sent shivers running through her, banishing the ecstasy of his lovemaking.

'You were a virgin,' he said flatly, and to her it sounded like an accusation. She felt her face grow hot and he laughed. 'You'll have to grow out of that habit now you're no longer an innocent.'

'You never thought I was,' Claudia said sadly. She had just had the most beautiful experience of her whole life and Roman was looking at her as if she had cheated him.

'I'm sorry if it wasn't any good for you,' she whispered.

'I didn't say that,' he mocked. 'It was very good, but you should have told me—then again, perhaps that was the idea.'

'Idea of what?' Claudia didn't like this Roman; he

had changed with bewildering speed from her lover to a man who was withdrawing more and more from her with every word he uttered.

'Perhaps I'm doing you an injustice,' he said, swinging his legs over the side of the bed, his back to her. 'Perhaps you're not trying for the prize of a wedding-ring; if so, I apologise, though nothing can bring back what I've taken from you.'

'You took nothing I didn't want to give,' she said, wishing she could see his face. 'I'm not trying for a wedding-ring or anything else; I'll put it down to experience, so you have no need to be afraid of my intentions, or to reproach yourself.' She slid from the bed and picked up her robe, belting it tightly round her. She had his attention now and she wasn't sure she liked it.

'That's how you want to play it, is it?' he asked, coming quickly towards her. 'I don't agree with you—we have something very special, and if you don't want a wedding-ring we can deal well together.' He put his hands on her shoulders, towering over her, his powerful body so compelling that she thought she would fall if he let her go.

It would be so easy to say yes to everything he was asking of her; she wouldn't have his love but she would have his arms round her all through the nights that, from now on, promised to be lonely.

'Well?' he murmured. 'You know what I want; come to me, Gemini girl—you won't regret it, I promise.'

He couldn't know what an effort it was to push him away. As for regret, she was feeling that already, but how much sharper it would be when he decided he didn't want her any more, as he certainly would do sooner or later.

'No, Roman, it wouldn't work.'

'Why not?' he said, not moving an inch. His hands tightened when she tried to step back, and Claudia, refusing a struggle that could only lead to one thing, stood very still.

'I don't fancy being anyone's mistress, any more than you fancy being a husband.'

'There is a difference.'

'Yes, there is; it's easier to walk away from a girlfriend when the time comes.'

'It is, but why look so far ahead? There could be many glorious months in front of us before that time comes.' Claudia twisted away from him, conscious that if he wanted to keep her close to him she hadn't a chance.

'The answer is still no.' He lifted his hands from her shoulders and raised an indifferent eyebrow. 'I can only go along with you, but I'm still asking you not to leave until Dana does. I'd rather not have any more scenes.'

'Dana would be happier if I did leave,' Claudia said, knowing she spoke the truth. A sharp pang shot through her at the thought of Dana travelling alone with Roman.

'I wouldn't,' he said grimly. 'Please, Claudia, do this for me.' She found herself agreeing weakly as he kissed her, pulling her into his arms as if he had every right. She pushed her hands against his chest but he held her effortlessly, laughing down into her upturned face.

'It's no use struggling against the inevitable,

Claudia. Deny it as much as you like, but we're
lovers now and shall continue to be so.' Claudia
fought hard against her traitorous body that already
acknowledged him as its master, trying to hold
herself away from him. Roman lowered his head and
his mouth closed over hers.

The door opened abruptly, and over Roman's
shoulder Claudia saw Dana stop short in confusion.
Roman brushed Claudia's lips with his and, still
holding her close, looked calmly at Dana.

'Did you want me, Dana?' Claudia said, wincing
at the contempt in her twin's eyes.

'Not you—I want Roman.' Dana made her intentions very clear and she wasn't to be turned from her
objective by the sight of Roman kissing Claudia.

'As you can see, Dana, we're busy, and it is
customary to knock on bedroom doors.' Claudia
would have shrivelled at the note in Roman's voice,
but Dana only laughed and put her hand on his arm.

'I'm bored, and I didn't think you wanted me to
return to London by myself.'

'There's no need for you to do that, Dana—you
can come with us,' Claudia said firmly. Dana looked
shocked; Claudia had never spoken to her in that
tone before.

'That's right, we were just going to pack but we
got waylaid.' Claudia blushed, and Roman kissed
the tip of her nose.

'You can help Claudia, Dana, and then we'll
collect your things from the hotel, though you seem
to have bought a fresh wardrobe.' He raised an
eyebrow at the parcels she had dropped just inside
the door, and Claudia blushed again, this time for

her sister. How could she spend Roman's money so lavishly when she had just parted from her lover?

'Why not? He gave it me to spend, presumably so he could spend time making love to you, sister, dear,' Dana said when Claudia asked her that question after Roman had gone to his room.

Claudia held on to her temper with an effort; it was bad enough that Dana had leapt to the right conclusion without her confirming it.

'Roman did make love to you while I was spending his money, didn't he?' Dana persisted.

'That's my business, Dana. You still have no right to spend money that isn't yours.'

'He'll never miss it—he's loaded.' She pulled a shimmering gold evening dress out of a box and held it in front of her, gazing into the long mirror as if she loved the combination of woman and gown. As she did, Claudia realised, pity mixing wth sorrow as she remembered that Dana had just parted with the man she loved.

'I'm sorry about you and Garry; it must be torture for you to lose him, but his wife and child must come first,' she said sympathetically. Dana shrugged shapely shoulders and, folding the gold dress carefully back into its box, opened another. This one held a dark blue chiffon trouser suit, highly impractical, but it would suit Dana perfectly.

'Don't let it worry you; Garry and I had fun while it lasted, but Roman is worth ten of him. I'm sure he's an exciting lover, and he has far more money than Garry, *and* he isn't married.' She slanted a challenging look at Claudia. 'I don't count his little side-step with you; that's neither here nor there.'

She discarded the trouser suit for a set of underwear in palest pink, and Claudia seethed at having the most wonderful moments of her life dismissed in so summary a fashion.

'I'm giving you fair warning, Claudia, that I'm taking Roman Wyatt from you. He's wasted on you, while I will treasure him.'

'You'll treasure what he can give you, you mean,' Claudia said grimly.

'How right you are, but I'll also give good value for every penny. If I read him right he doesn't intend to marry, so he wouldn't suit you, would he?' She paused, stroking the soft satin camiknickers. 'I might even change his mind about marriage. A model has a short career, and a husband like Roman Wyatt would have compensations, as I'm sure you agree. Don't look so shocked, Claudia—he'd never marry you; you wouldn't fit in with his lifestyle and he'd be bored out of his mind in a month.'

'I think Roman will decide for himself, Dana, and I don't believe his plans include marriage to anyone.' Roman's early experience had altered him irrevocably from a loving young man to a hard cynic who would never let any other woman near enough to win his love and trust.

'You could be right, sister dear, but a man in his position needs a wife, and I would fit in with him in every way. I mean it, Claudia, and if you're wise you'll stay out of my way.'

CHAPTER EIGHT

THE journey home was, to say the least, uncomfortable. Dana sulked because Roman had thwarted her
plan to sit in the front passenger seat, and Claudia,
conscious of her twin's glowering presence, couldn't
find anything to say. Roman, on his part, was equally
silent, and it was with relief that Claudia recognised
the outskirts of Solihull. Dana sat up, her bored
expression changing to one of indignation.

'I don't want to go to Solihull,' she said petulantly.
Then she smiled as a thought came to her. 'You're
dropping Claudia off here, of course, then you're
taking me on to London, aren't you, Roman?' He
shook his head, his eyes meeting Dana's in the
mirror.

'I'm not going to London, Dana; I don't want to
drive any further today and I have business here.
Like Claudia, I have an interest in the NEC show,
and it's time I checked on the progress of my
entries.'

'That won't take you long, surely? We can go to
London tomorrow—I'd much prefer to drive there
with you than go by train.' She smiled at him
beguilingly and Claudia felt sick. Dana was bewitch-
ing when she smiled like that and Roman didn't
seem at all annoyed by her persistence. Instead he
was smiling back at her.

'I'll think about it. My business could take more

than one day, but if you're not in a hurry. . .?' He
left the question in the air, and Claudia wasn't
surprised to see Dana's smile deepen.

'I can wait for you,' she said huskily, and Claudia
wanted nothing more than to leave a car that was
rapidly becoming far too small for three. Before long
Roman pulled up outside Claudia's flat. He got out
and helped her from her seat, and turned to do the
same for Dana.

'Dana can stay with you, Claudia——' he began,
and Dana pouted.

'Claudia's flat is so small—can't I stay in your
hotel with you, Roman?'

'I'm staying with a friend and it's even more
cramped than your sister's flat,' he said politely, and
Claudia repressed a smile; Denzil's flat had plenty of
room, but she was glad Roman didn't want to share
it with Dana. Roman turned to Claudia, but she
refused to respond to the message he was silently
trying to convey.

'We have things to discuss, Claudia; I'll see you
tomorrow.' He dropped a kiss on her cheek, lifted
his hand to Dana, and strode back to his car.

Dana darted after him but Roman didn't appear
to notice her, or to hear her calling him, and she
could only watch as he drove away. Claudia also
watched him go; then she walked into the flat,
wishing she were on her own. Dana wasn't the
easiest flatmate on record, and now that she was
upset by Roman's refusal to take her with him she
would be impossible.

Her fears were justified during the next few hours,
and Claudia was relieved when Dana at last went to

sleep, curled up in Claudia's spare bed, her rumpled curls damp with angry tears.

Claudia straightened the cover over her twin; she loved Dana dearly, but there were times when she had to admit her sister was a trial. If she hadn't known her twin better, Dana's mask of sophistication could have wounded her deeply, particularly when she persisted in being so sure that Roman would do exactly as she wished. She turned into her own room and, discarding her clothes, slipped into bed.

Images of Roman and the time they had made love swam before her closed eyes. He had been everything she had ever imagined the man she loved would be. Somehow in the days they had spent together he had twined himself within her heart and soul so completely that there was no denying he was there to stay. If she had nurtured any hope of forgetting him one day in the future his lovemaking had banished that hope forever.

Even if she never saw him again, even if he married Dana, she was his for the rest of her life. He might just as well have branded her with the seal of his possession.

A tear found its way from under her eyelid, sliding down her cheek. She wiped it hastily away; Roman wasn't hers to keep and, though he paid little attention to Dana, she was determined to have her own way, and Claudia knew that what Dana wanted she usually got.

Dana wanted to marry Roman and on her own showing she would make a far more suitable wife for him than her twin would. Claudia sat upright, all thought of sleep discarded. She was damned if she would give in so easily. For a moment the light of battle glowed in her eyes, dying as she remembered that Roman didn't love her.

She lay down again and resolutely set her mind on sleep, with such good effect that she knew no more until a hand on her shoulder woke her. It was still early, as she could tell from the light filtering through her curtains, and she narrowed her eyes at the sight of a cross Dana, who was obviously prepared to shake her again.

'What is it?' she mumbled sleepily. 'Is there anything wrong? Oh, it's not Berenice, is it?'

'Nothing is wrong, and as far as I know Berenice is still in one piece. I've had a dreadful night, Claudia, and I want my coffee.'

'Try the kitchen,' Claudia said, seeing from the clock on her bedside table that there was an hour before she needed to get up.

'I thought you'd make it for me,' Dana faltered; usually Claudia would leap to do her twin's bidding, but this morning she told her where the coffee lived, turned her back and went back to sleep.

The alarm clock woke Claudia for the second time and she sniffed appreciatively at the aroma penetrating her room. She showered, and dressed in a pale grey cotton skirt with a crisp white blouse, brushed her hair into its customery neat knot, used her cosmetics sparingly and walked into the kitchen, looking the picture of a successful businesswoman. Dana, slumped over the kitchen table in a bright pink robe that left little to the imagination, raised resentful eyes.

'So you've decided to surface, and about time—you can make fresh coffee; I've finished the pot I made earlier.' Claudia started more coffee, reflecting that if Dana was going to stay for any length of time she would need fresh supplies. She put her usual slice of bread into the toaster, raising her eyebrows in enquiry.

'Not for me—I don't eat breakfast. I have to watch my figure. . . I can't afford to get fat, not like you—a stone or so overweight won't matter in a shop, will it?'

Claudia, a smile curving her mouth, buttered her toast and sat down to eat. She wasn't going to let Dana provoke her; she weighed exactly the same as her twin and always had. Dana met her eyes and laughed.

'All right, I know you don't have an ounce more than I do, though you should, sitting at a desk all day.'

'Talking of desks, it's high time I was behind mine. Are you coming with me, Dana? The dress is ready for fitting.' Dana toyed with a golden curl, flicking it back over her shoulder.

'I want to see Roman first. What's the address of this place where he's staying?' Claudia's eyes darkened with amusement. Did Dana really think she would tell her? Meeting her twin's eyes, she knew she did. Dana had a blind spot where her own interests lay.

'If Roman wants to see you he knows where you are,' she said quietly.

'In other words, you won't tell me—if, that is, you know.' Claudia's amusement deepened; Dana was trying every trick she knew, but she wasn't about to fall into her trap.

'Why should I know?' she said, washing her mug and plate before putting them away. She ignored Dana's used mug; her twin would have plenty of time to wash up after herself.

'No reason you should—you're not Roman's type, are you, Claudia? You'd bore him out of his mind in a very short time.' That was probably true, but none the less painful. Claudia fetched her bag and jacket from her bedroom and, saying a quiet goodbye, left the flat.

She walked the short distance to work, seeing nothing of the beauty of the day. Early-morning sun was already gilding the leaves of the trees lining the streets, and women dressed in colourful summer clothes were taking their children to school.

For a few minutes she indulged in a fantasy where she was one of the young mothers and the child by her side was Roman's.

'I didn't expect to see you,' Myra said as Claudia walked through the showroom door.

'I should have phoned but the last few days have been so hectic that I didn't have time,' Claudia said as she gave Myra a brief account of finding Dana. Myra and Dreams had been pushed to the back of her mind. Roman and only Roman had filled her thoughts, to the exclusion of everything else.

'I wouldn't remember me either if I had a man like Roman Wyatt at my beck and call,' Myra said, grinning as Claudia blushed.

'I'm not involved with Mr Wyatt,' Claudia said, walking quickly into her office, where she settled at her desk with a determined look on her face. Myra shrugged her shoulders and found something to do that would keep her busy and well out of Claudia's way.

Dana sauntered into Claudia's office during the afternoon. She demanded to know where Roman was, and it was quite clear she didn't believe Claudia when she said she didn't know.

'He said he'd see you today,' Dana said, perching on the edge of Claudia's desk, scattering the designs she had been working on, much to her annoyance.

'He hasn't so far,' Claudia said, putting down her pencil.

'If he wants to see either of us he will, but I've no doubt he is as busy as I am,' she added pointedly. Dana ignored her sister's pin-prick and, taking a mirror from her bag, scrutinised her perfect complexion with minute care.

'If he doesn't come soon I'm off to London,' she said, running a finger over one arched eyebrow. Alarm flared up in Claudia; that was the last thing Roman wanted. She felt a moment of irritation—trust a man to absent himself and leave her to keep Dana away from London and Garry.

'I'd be grateful if you could spare time for a fitting, and I did think it would be a good idea if I could hold a rehearsal of everyone concerned in my part of the show before the official one. I know it must seem an unnecessary fuss to you, Dana, but it's a big opportunity for me and I want everything to be as perfect as possible,' she said urgently. Dana looked at her twin and laughed.

'I don't doubt that, Claudia, but you also want to

keep me away from Garry,' she added shrewdly, 'and you want even more to keep me away from Roman. Well, you can't have it both ways. You can tell him from me that if he wants me to stay in this urban backwater of yours he'll have to provide me with an interesting occupation—and I don't mean modelling your dress. As for the rehearsal, I'll consider it tomorrow. Right now I'm going to see if there's anything decent to wear in this town.'

She strolled gracefully out of the office, and Claudia admired her poise, while condemning her attitude. Dana thought everyone should do just as she wanted, and why not? Most people usually did. The telephone rang a few minutes later, and she came to life as Roman's deep voice answered her.

'Claudia, is Dana there?' he asked, and her happy anticipation died at birth.

'You've just missed her,' she said quietly. An angry exclamation made her wince.

'I should have phoned earlier, but I was tied up.'

'Can I give her a message?'

'Not really, I just thought she might be getting restless and I've had an idea. It's no use my telling you what it is—she might not agree, and then it would only be a waste of time.' Claudia swallowed bitter disappointment; Roman didn't even care enough about her to confide in her, even when his plan concerned her sister.

'Dana is fed up with Solihull and she's already thinking about going back to London.' There was nothing Claudia would have liked more than for Dana to put distance between herself and Roman, but for Berenice's sake she mustn't be allowed to divert Garry's attention away from his wife.

'That mustn't happen—where is she, do you know?'

'Gone shopping,' Claudia said sharply, relenting at the anxious note in Roman's voice as he asked how long she would be. 'The shops here are very good, but Dana is inclined to turn her nose up at anything outside London or Paris, so I imagine an hour could see her back at the flat.'

'Right; I'll try there. . .thanks, Claudia,' and the phone went dead before she could say anything more. That's put you in your place, my girl; Roman hadn't even enquired how she was—their love-making had already vanished into limbo as far as he was concerned. Claudia felt an overwhelming sadness. She loved him so much, and to realise that she was only an episode in his busy life was bitter indeed.

He had asked her to live with him, or had he? Perhaps he only meant them to meet when he could fit her in with his other engagements. She felt a bubble of hysteria rising in her throat and took a deep breath. It was all academic anyway. Roman was intent on making sure her twin didn't stray back to Garry, and, with Dana ready and willing to co-operate with him, Claudia didn't stand a chance.

She deliberately stayed late, working long after a disapproving Myra had said goodnight, and only giving up when she was too tired to see the design she was working on.

She walked slowly through the quiet streets, won-dering if Dana and Roman would be cosily together in her flat. She needn't have worried; a brief note

from Dana on the kitchen table said that Roman
was taking her out to dinner and that she was not to
wait up, neither was she to wake Dana in the
morning; she would come for her fitting in the
afternoon.

That set the pattern for the next few days. Claudia
hardly saw Dana; she left in the morning before her
twin left her room, though more than once Claudia
heard her moving about and she knew Dana was
deliberately waiting until she left the flat before
appearing to drink the coffee left ready for her.

Dana didn't come to the showroom either; she
had appeared for a fitting and for a rehearsal, as she
had promised, neither of which had been an outstanding success. Claudia had wanted more fittings
and Dana had promised that she would fit them in,
but time passed and the dress still hung, swathed in
its wrappings, awaiting her pleasure.

She had always left the flat by the time Claudia
came home, and she knew her sister was with
Roman, and the dull despair that lived with her
permanently would deepen a little more as she tidied
the theatre programmes or the menu from an exclusive restaurant. She didn't need telling who
Dana's companion had been, or that the menu had
been left for her to find.

Claudia sat behind her desk and looked at the date
to which Myra had just drawn her attention.

'It's the second of July,' she said in horror; 'the
show is only ten days away.'

'That's what I've been trying to tell you,' Myra
said. 'I realise something is wrong, and I don't have

to look too far to know the cause,' she added darkly, 'but you must get down to work or the show will be a failure, and you don't want that to happen, do you?'

Claudia looked into Myra's anxious face and tried to smile. 'I don't seem to care very much, Myra, but you're right—I do want the show to succeed; so many people have worked so hard that I can't let them down.'

'I never thought I'd hear you say you didn't care about your designs.'

Claudia put her hand on Myra's arm. 'Neither did I, and I do care, Myra, really I do, it's just. . .' She sat back, unable to continue.

'You've fallen in love with Roman Wyatt, haven't you?' Myra said softly. 'And that man-eating sister of yours is determined to have him herself, isn't she?' Myra's down-to-earth remarks made Claudia smile weakly.

'Dana isn't really a man-eater; she only wants to be happy.'

'She doesn't care if she pushes everyone, including you, aside in her efforts to achieve it either,' Myra said with disgust. 'And you still haven't answered my question. You do love him, don't you?'

Claudia nodded, unable to put into words her intense love and longing for Roman.

'I thought so, but what I can't understand is why you're letting Dana get away with it. I know she's your twin, but that doesn't mean you should give her the man you want. Geminis have dual personalities and I think you have the best part of their nature, while Dana has the rotten bits.'

'Don't say that, Myra; Dana has many good qualities.'

'Where?' Myra muttered.

'Perhaps Roman is just what Dana needs to bring them out,' Claudia said. 'There was a time when I intended to fight—perhaps I still would if I thought I had a chance and if I ever saw either of them, but it's hard to fight for a man as elusive as Roman has become.'

'Haven't you seen him at all?' Myra sounded shocked. Claudia had gone away with him, and to Myra's romantic mind it must have been a foregone conclusion that they would become lovers and live happily ever after. They had become lovers, but as for the rest. . .

'I did see him briefly three days ago.' Claudia closed her eyes as she remembered the time she had come home earlier than usual. Dana had still been in the bathroom getting ready for her evening with Roman. The doorbell had shrilled, and Dana had popped her head round the bathroom door.

'Answer that, Claudia, and tell Roman I won't be a moment.' She withdrew, and Claudia opened the door, steeling herself to greet Roman without a trace of the emotion that made her want to run out of the flat, away from the two people she loved most and who were causing her so much pain that she wanted to die.

She gave Roman Dana's message in a monotone that revealed far more than she knew. Roman winced as he took in her fragile appearance, and Claudia, on her part, wondered why he didn't look either well or happy, while Dana was positively blooming.

The lines from his nose to his mouth were deeper, his mouth was set in a grim line and his eyes were bleak, or perhaps her memory was at fault. . .but she knew it wasn't; she knew every inch of his face. Colour washed into her cheeks as she recalled that his face wasn't the only part of him she knew.

'You're blushing,' Roman said quietly. He stretched out a hand to touch her face and she jerked away. He mustn't touch her or she would shatter to pieces, fall on him and ask him why he was ignoring her in favour of her sister.

She didn't need to ask; there was an aura about Dana that made Claudia feel she was a grey shadow of her twin. There was also that necessity of keeping Dana happy and away from London, but, even so, Roman didn't have to ignore her own existence to such an extent. An expression of pain crossed his face at Claudia's reaction. He didn't attempt to touch her again, but he stood squarely in front of her, thwarting her attempts to escape.

'Dana should be ready now; I'll tell her you're waiting,' she said, wanting only to gain the privacy of her room, where she could release the tears that were threatening.

'Forget Dana for a moment—she's not important,' Roman said urgently.

'Important enough for you to take her out every night,' Claudia responded, gasping as she realised she had spoken her thoughts out loud.

'So you do care?' His expression changed, and he

would have taken her in his arms if she hadn't
moved quickly.

'I care that you're trying to seduce Dana as you
seduced me. . .nothing more, though I doubt your
conceit will allow you to believe that.' The light in
his eyes dimmed and his arms fell to his sides.

'I hoped you would trust me, but obviously you
can't,' he said, anger making his voice hard. 'As it
is, I have nothing to lose.' He seized her and brought
his mouth down on hers in a punishing kiss that
made her senses swim. She fought free, but she had
no time to tell him just what she thought of a man
who would play one sister against the other before
Dana was in the room.

Dana was beautiful in an outrageous red gown
that looked magnificent. She brushed past Claudia,
and with a muttered goodnight swept Roman with
her out of the flat.

'Well, what happened?' Myra's eager question
banished Claudia's memory of that painful meeting.
She straightened and, running her hand over her
neat hair, smiled at Myra.

'Not much; he said he hoped I would trust him.'

'There you are, then,' Myra crowed. 'Everything
will turn out fine, take my word.'

'I wish I could, Myra, but I've finally stopped
believing in fairy-tales.' She got up briskly. 'It's also
time I got down to thinking positively about this
show. Ring the flat, will you, Myra, and ask. . .no,
tell Dana we expect her here in an hour for a
rehearsal? On second thoughts, *I'll* ring Dana—you
muster the rest of the models.'

She drew the phone towards her and Myra grinned

in relief. Claudia was at last putting her unhappiness to one side and was ready to concentrate on the all-important show.

Claudia could hear the phone ringing on and on in her flat. She put the phone down thoughtfully. It wasn't like Dana to be out before noon. When she had the chance she took hours over her beauty treatment.

Further phone calls during the day produced the same result, and by four-thirty Claudia was getting worried. She seized her jacket and bag, said a few words to Myra and practically ran the short distance to her flat, visions of Dana lying unconscious from a fall filling her mind.

CHAPTER NINE

THE flat was empty. Claudia drew a deep breath; Dana must have left hours ago. Her room was in its usual chaotic state and her used coffee-mug was still on the table. Claudia sat on a stool, relief pouring through her. Much as she resented her all-out pursuit of Roman, Dana was the sister she had loved all her life.

It wasn't Dana's fault if Roman preferred her to her twin; he had wanted Claudia, but once had been enough. He had never pretended to love her and it was her misfortune that the time that had meant nothing to him had made him hers forever.

It wasn't any use going back to the shop now; she would phone Myra, then she would get down to designing the bridesmaids' dresses that would match the bride's gown she was commissioned to make for a big wedding in the autumn.

Claudia looked at her drawing with dissatisfaction. It wasn't up to her usual standard—she would have to start again. Perhaps if she had something to eat it would help her to concentrate. She glanced at her watch; nine o'clock. Where was Dana? All her fears rushed back. Something was wrong; she should have listened to her instincts, not allowed herself to be lulled into a false security by the normal appearance of the flat.

Roman; he must know where Dana was. She

stretched out her hand to the phone when she heard a key in the door. She rushed out into the hall as the door swung open and a pale, rumpled Dana walked in, followed closely by Roman.

'Dana; what's happened?' Claudia said, rushing to her twin. Dana fended her off, stalking past her into the living-room.

'I told you Claudia would know, she always does; it's as if she lives in my head.' Her tone was sharp but the eyes that met Claudia's were vulnerable; then she sat down and laughed. 'Cheer up, Claudia, it's nothing; I'm perfectly all right.'

Are you? Claudia asked silently. Dana had been badly shaken; her clothes were dusty and there was a tear in the red shorts she was wearing.

Shorts; Dana hated the things—they offended the dignity of which she was so proud. Claudia took in the rest of Dana's clothes, her eyes wide with astonishment. A pink T-shirt with the slogan 'I like A Sporting Man' sprawled across the front moulded Dana's figure closely, her hair was covered by a silk scarf printed with tennis players, and chunky earrings completed an outfit far removed from anything she had seen her sister wear before. Dana put her hand to the scarf and patted it.

'It stayed in place,' she said in amazement.

'So it did, as it was meant to do, but I didn't expect or want such a drastic test.'

'It's a special design of Roman's—it's supposed to stay put, even in a strong wind,' Dana said, her high voice telling Claudia she wasn't as calm as she would like to appear.

'Will someone tell me what is going on?' Claudia

said firmly. Dana had been hurt, or at least scared, and all she and Roman could talk about was a wretched headscarf.

'Keep your hair on, sister mine; I've had my feathers ruffled, but that's all,' Dana said, pulling the scarf off her head.

'Dana has had a slight accident,' Roman said, his deep voice expressing his concern.

'Accident!' Dana snorted. 'Some accident; I was deliberately pushed off that catwalk and you know it.'

'Who would do such a thing?' Claudia demanded indignantly.

'Your sister isn't best known for her tact; she had just informed one of the other models that she was too fat to wear shorts. It was an impulsive reaction on Teresa's part and one I'm sure won't be repeated.'

'It had better not be,' Dana said curtly. 'I should refuse to work with that rotten cow.'

'You won't refuse, though, will you?' Roman said almost casually and Claudia was astonished to see her twin bite her lip and lower her eyes.

'I can guarantee it won't happen again, but you must try to fit in, Dana. I know you're a top model but the others have their pride and it doesn't do to trample all over them.' To Claudia's amazement Dana raised repentant eyes to him and smiled. He smiled back, and Claudia felt a shaft of pain shoot through her. It was so strong that she put a hand to her head and swayed. In an instant Roman was beside her, his arm round her waist.

'Dana, get some water—Claudia's going to faint,' he ordered.

'No, I'm quite all right.' Claudia moved away from him quickly. In another moment she would have collapsed against him. It was so perfect, so right to be in his arms. All she wanted to do was to snuggle close to him, but waves of resentment coming from Dana told her that was the last thing she could do.

'I still don't understand. What was Dana doing on a catwalk?'

'Don't you know?'

'I don't tell Claudia everything,' Dana said sulkily. 'And I am conscious—you don't have to talk over my head.'

'In that case, tell me what you were doing modelling shorts when you should have been rehearsing with the wedding dress you're to wear at the show.'

'I'm sure you've guessed by now. I've been rehearsing the sports clothes I'll also be wearing at the NEC.' Claudia sat down quickly, feeling she would fall if she didn't.

'Let me get this straight; you're going to model clothes for Roman?'

'Correct, and, before you start on about your precious dress, I can do both.'

'Are you sure?' Roman said quietly. 'I'm sorry, Claudia, I didn't know Dana was committed to you.'

'I'm not,' Dana said swiftly. 'Claudia's dress is right at the end—I shall have plenty of time.'

Claudia sighed; Dana in this mood couldn't be reasoned with. She had a point; the sports clothes were in the first part of the programme—there should be time for her to change into the wedding dress for the finale.

'I'm going to have a bath. I don't want to stiffen up or I won't be able to model anything.' Dana flounced out of the room, confident she had everything arranged to her satisfaction.

'I didn't know Dana was modelling one of your dresses, Claudia. She was delighted when I asked her to work for me,' Roman said, his voice warm with sympathy.

'I'm sure she was—your name is famous and it will help her career to model your clothes,' Claudia said stiffly. He sat down so close to her that every nerve in her body came to vibrant life.

'I would release her but it's important to keep her happy, although I'm sorry it's turned out like this.' Claudia wanted to believe he was sincere, but something held her back.

'Are you certain Dana didn't drop a hint about my dress?' she asked. Roman wrinkled his brows.

'She could have done. I must plead guilty to not listening very intently to everything Dana says.' He reached for her hand, holding it closely in his warm grasp. 'I have a very good reason for wanting Dana close to me. Will you try to trust me, Claudia?' Claudia withdrew her hand from his.

'Why should I trust you? You aren't about to explain, are you?' Her hope that he would say it was for Berenice's sake died as soon as it was born. Roman frowned but didn't answer, and Claudia stood up; she couldn't bear sitting so close to the man she loved and had lost to her sister any longer.

'How is your sister?' she said abruptly.

'Holding her own, just,' Roman said, and Claudia heard his relief at the change of subject with resignation. There was nothing so dead as an old love, and what they had shared had only been desire on his part. It had been very different for her but he couldn't be held responsible for her folly.

'Claudia,' he said urgently, and jumped to his feet and pulled her hard against him. 'I can't stand you looking so sad. There's nothing you can't know. I've asked Dana to——'

'Claudia.' Dana's shrill voice made Claudia jump away from Roman as if she were guilty of something, but Roman had only been about to say he had asked Dana to model for him in order to get to know her better. Oh, surely he hadn't been going to say he had asked her twin to marry him?

Claudia looked at Dana's angry face and knew that if Roman had proposed she would have told her, triumphantly, as soon as she had seen her, accident or no accident. Her rapidly beating heart steadied and she answered Dana calmly.

'Did you want me, Dana?' Her twin shot a glance at Roman before answering Claudia.

'Yes, I want you to stay with me while I have a bath. I'm so stiff that I'm afraid of slipping when I get out, and you can help me wash my hair—my arms hurt when I lift them up.' That could be true, but on the other hand Dana wouldn't want to leave Claudia with Roman for any length of time, and she was right, wasn't she? Roman had been holding her in his arms and she hadn't been fighting—no wonder Dana was furious.

She turned to the bathroom, throwing Roman a

quiet goodnight over her shoulder. Dana took her time in following her sister, and Claudia imagined she would take full advantage of her sister's absence.

Claudia ran Dana's bath, testing the water carefully. She shouldn't blame her twin; Roman had said he wanted Dana close to him, and who could wonder if her did? Even when she had just fallen from a catwalk, Dana had a vivacity Claudia couldn't match. She heard the outer door close and a moment later Dana stormed into the bathroom.

'Well, that was a nice little scene I interrupted,' she said, glaring at Claudia as if she was her mortal enemy. Claudia raised the bottle of shampoo in mute enquiry. Dana was best left unanswered in her present mood. As she had hoped, the shampoo diverted Dana's thoughts.

'I can't use that stuff,' she said in horror. 'I've got my own.' She darted into her bedroom and reappeared with a cut-glass bottle of a very expensive make.

Claudia obediently washed Dana's thick hair as she sat in the bath, sniffing appreciatively at the perfume that floated round her twin. Dana loved luxury and she seemed to manage to surround herself with things Claudia couldn't even dream of buying.

'That's better,' Dana said as Claudia dried her hair.

'Are you very stiff, Dana?'

'Not now. I'll be able to model your gown; it's right at the end of the show, so I'll have a few minutes after I've finished Roman's clothes.'

'How many outfits, apart from mine, are you

modelling?' Claudia asked, her heart sinking at the idea of Dana rushing from shorts into a wedding dress in the space of a few minutes.

'All Roman's most important new designs—six or seven in all.'

'That many? I know you think I'm making a fuss, Dana, but this is my first time at a major show and the finale is important.'

'It's all important; Roman is the foremost designer of sports and leisure clothes in the world, and you must realise he can do a great deal for my career.'

'In other words, my gown is unimportant compared to shorts with Roman's name on them.'

'You said it.' Dana tilted her head back and looked at her sister. 'There could be more than just a career,' she said softly. 'Oh, I know I've been a trial to you ever since Mother died, and running away with Garry wasn't the smartest thing I've ever done, but at least I met Roman because I was foolish and I don't think he'll hold it against me, will he?' All at once she looked and sounded uncertain and very much the sister Claudia had always loved. 'Please say Roman won't hold Garry against me; oh, please say he won't,' she pleaded, tears falling from her beautiful eyes, and Claudia, as always, couldn't resist her.

'No, of course he won't,' she said. 'Roman is far too much of a man to do that.'

'That's what I thought,' Dana said, mopping her eyes with a corner of the towel. She was happy now; Claudia had confirmed her own hopes. 'He's a Sagittarius, and Sagittarius and Gemini are good together.'

'I thought you didn't believe in that kind of thing.'

'I don't, I just happened to see that tatty book of horoscopes Myra keeps on her desk while I was waiting for you one day, so I looked it up,' Dana said defiantly. 'You believe in it, so I wanted to know what it was all about.'

'I don't know whether I believe the stars rule our destiny or not, but I do think twins have a special bond,' Claudia said. Dana refused to look at her and walked out of the bathroom.

'That's as maybe; we're not a bit alike, sister dear, so your theory falls flat. My hair's dry now; can I have a hot drink, please? I must get a good night's sleep.' She got into bed and settled back against the pillows. She was in command once more, all traces of her weak, dependent side hidden. Claudia smiled ruefully as she poured skimmed milk into a pan. Dana could put on a good show; no one would know she had broken down and confessed her need for Roman's strength.

Her twin must love Roman very much to have let Claudia know how worried she was about his reaction to her escapade with Garry. She gave Dana her drink and turned to go, but Dana called her back.

'Don't go for a moment, Claudia. I know you think I've been casual about your gown, but when Roman insisted I wear his clothes I couldn't turn him down, could I?' She turned wide, appealing eyes to her sister, and Claudia knew very few men would be able to resist her. 'I'm wearing outfits not only for active sports but for all kinds of leisure activities,' Dana said, heedless of Claudia's strained silence.

'What are you showing just before the finale?'

'Disco gear; we have the most fantastic make-up and we dance along the catwalk to the most way-out music, which Roman has had specially composed.' She frowned. 'It would be better if it were less strenuous, but don't worry, your display will be fine.'

Would it? Claudia lay sleepless, visions of Dana jiving at the head of the bridal procession, dressed in shorts and a veil instead of the lovely dress Claudia had spent so much time designing, going through her head.

She turned on her side; it wasn't the show that worried her as much as the thought of Dana and Roman working so closely together. He expected her to trust him, but as far as she could see they were just empty words. If he loved Dana he would be part of her sister's life and she hoped she would never have to see him again.

The next few days slipped away like sand through her fingers. Claudia felt as if she were running hard to remain in the same place. There were only three days now before the show and things were not going smoothly.

Dana had not appeared for the promised fitting or for the rehearsal, excusing herself at the last minute because Roman had wanted her for alterations to one of the outfits she was to wear. Claudia reluctantly took her place while Myra concentrated on last-minute adjustments.

'Your measurements are exactly the same as Dana's and the dress suits you even better—you could easily wear it on the day.'

'I couldn't; I should die of fright,' Claudia said,

alarmed at the very thought of walking on stage in full view of an audience. 'How can you say it suits me more than it does Dana? As you've pointed out, our measurements are the same and we look alike.'

'You may do, but there's an aura about you Dana has lost.'

'I know what you mean. I'm a country girl, Dana is a sophisticated beauty, and it shows.'

'It certainly does; you have the advantage over your sister every time.'

'Thank you for those kind words, Myra. . .you wouldn't be the least bit prejudiced, would you?'

'No more than anyone else who knows you both. I can't understand why Roman Wyatt has turned his attentions to Dana, and I don't like the way he's stolen her from us.'

'You can't blame either of them. It's a marvellous chance for Dana, and Roman obviously recognises that she's an outstanding model.'

'Outstanding my foot,' Myra said, jabbing a pin into Claudia's leg in her indignation.

'That's me!' Claudia squealed, and Myra apologised, looking far more upset than Claudia was. An hour later Claudia lifted the phone, spoke soothingly to the woman at the other end and replaced the receiver, her face grim.

'What's wrong?' Myra asked as she came into the office carrying a mug of tea.

'It was Mrs Hardcastle—Alison has a nasty attack of flu, and she won't be fit enough to wear the chief bridesmaid's dress on Saturday.'

Myra flopped down on the nearest chair. 'Oh, lord; what do we do now?'

'We can only try the agency. We can't hope for anyone with Alison's exact measurements, but do the best you can.' She lifted the receiver as Myra darted to the other phone and, her mouth set in a straight line, dialled the number of Roman's office. All her pleas to Dana had gone unanswered. When cornered she had promised to come to the show-room, but when the time came there was no Dana and Claudia was lucky if she even got a flimsy excuse.

Dana was equally elusive at the flat; she was either out when Claudia returned home or in bed with the door locked and a note pinned to the handle saying she was very tired. Time was getting short; she must talk to Dana, and this time she was going right to the top. Roman answered the phone himself at the first ring, and Claudia's heart turned over.

It seemed a lifetime since they had made love but the mere sound of his deep voice brought it back so vividly that she shivered, aware that she wanted and loved him more than ever.

'Yes?' he said impatiently. 'Who is it?' and Claudia managed to say her name. 'Claudia!' His reply was a joyful shout that made her grip the receiver tightly. 'Claudia, I'm so glad you phoned. Does this mean you've forgiven me?'

'Forgiven you for what?' Claudia said, at a complete loss. What had he done that needed forgiveness, apart from falling in love with Dana? Love wasn't something you could give or withhold at will. 'I don't understand, Roman; as far as I know, there's nothing to forgive. I've phoned to ask your help.'

'Ask away,' he said, a puzzled note creeping into his voice.

'It's Dana; she promises to come for fittings and rehearsals but all I get are excuses. I'm sure you can't be keeping her so busy that she can't spare me an hour or so.' There was a silence so heavy that Claudia thought it would shatter the phone, and when he spoke his voice was cold and remote.

'There's something Dana hasn't told you that you should have known days ago, Claudia. I'll have to tell you myself; I'll come as soon as I can.'

The phone went dead and she stared at it as if it had bitten her. What was all that about? What should Dana have told her? She had known there was something wrong; Dana had been too determined to avoid her, and Claudia's finely tuned senses told her Dana was uneasy. She turned to the door as Myra came in, her smile saying she had been successful.

'The agency has a girl who sounds very possible— she'll be here at ten tomorrow morning.' Claudia smiled faintly.

'I'm glad something is going right.'

'No luck with Dana?' Myra asked sympathetically. Claudia shook her head.

'I didn't manage to speak to her,' she said elusively. The phone conversation with Roman had shaken her and she wanted to think about it before she said any more.

After Myra had returned to the showroom Claudia sat unmoving behind her desk, her mind in complete confusion. What was it Roman thought important enough for a visit? It was something to do with Dana; what wasn't so clear was why Roman should have sounded upset because Dana hadn't told her herself. Her fingers closed convulsively round the pencil she was holding. Could she have been right when she had thought, almost a week ago, that Roman was about to tell her he had asked Dana to marry him?

Claudia relaxed her fingers, letting the pencil drop to the desk. What a nasty creature she was—how could she be jealous of Dana? She rubbed her knuckles across stinging eyes. She loved Roman so much that she was jealous of the air he breathed. She would have to learn to live with it. What if she had thought he was beginning to care for her? She had made a mistake and would make many more before she was finished.

In the meantime she had a business to run and a show to prepare. With a great effort she immersed herself in her work and it wasn't until Myra put her head round the door that she realised how quickly the time had gone.

'Goodness, is it that time already?'

'It is; I thought I might not catch you.' Roman's deep voice made Myra step aside with a knowing smile. She called a cheery goodnight over her shoulder and the door closed behind her.

Roman came into the room and it seemed to shrink before his powerful personality. He was dressed in a dark suit with a gleaming white shirt and he looked every bit as magnificent in his role of business tycoon as he did in more casual clothes.

'You wanted to tell me something?' Claudia said, hardly daring to look at him for fear of betraying how much she loved him. Roman sat on a corner of her desk and looked at her with such a grave expression that she cried out in alarm.

'What is it, Roman—is anything wrong with Dana? No,' she answered herself. 'There can't be, or I would know.'

'Yes, you would, wouldn't you?' he said quietly.'You're very sensitive to Dana and her needs, aren't you, Claudia?'

'She's my twin—shouldn't I be aware of her?' Roman looked at her with compassion.

'It does you credit, and it's a pity Dana doesn't feel the same way about you.'

'She does,' Claudia said, quick to defend her twin. 'Of course she does; how can you say otherwise?'

'The facts speak for themselves; if Dana had any feelings for you she'd have refused my offer. How can you defend her, Claudia, when she's let you down so badly?'

'She hasn't. Oh, I shouldn't have phoned you; I might have known you'd make it seem as if I'm moaning. Dana has missed a few fittings, but the earth won't stop turning and I'm sure she'll turn up for the next one.' Claudia jumped up and put her hand on his, snatching it away as her nerves reacted as if she had touched a live wire. 'It will be best if you don't say anything to Dana. I'll see her this evening—in fact, I'll go home now and catch her before you take her out.'

Roman shook his head. 'That's not possible; Dana isn't at the flat.' Claudia stared at him blankly.

'Not at the flat? Then where is she?' Roman put his hands on her shoulders and turned her gently to face him.

'I'm sorry, Claudia; Dana was supposed to tell you last night. By now she'll be in Paris.' His words fell like stones into a deep well, dropping from view without leaving a mark on her conscious mind. She stared at him for a long moment before she took in what he had said.

'Paris?' she whispered. 'Dana is in Paris? How can she be? The show is on Saturday and it's Wednesday now. Oh, how silly of her to take a holiday now; she'll have to return almost before she's got there and she'll be so tired. How could you let her go? She'd have listened to you.'

'She did—that's why she's gone. I've arranged for her to work in my Paris branch. We have a big promotion of leisure wear by top French designers; it's a chance of a lifetime for any model and one Dana couldn't miss once she knew about it.'

Claudia stared at him disbelievingly. He had deliberately sent Dana away when he must know how important it was she wear the gown designed for her. She became aware, too late, that she had spoken her thoughts out loud. Roman tightened his grip on her shoulders.

'It must seem like that, Claudia, and I admit I didn't think about your gown.' He paused and she pushed his hands away from her with a violence that she felt right through her. She was hurt, more than she believed possible, to know that Roman regarded her work so lightly that he could throw an elephant-sized spanner in her path without even thinking.

CHAPTER TEN

'WHY?' Claudia choked. 'Why send Dana to Paris now? If you didn't think of what it would mean to me, what about the clothes she was supposed to model for you?'

'My entry for the show consists mostly of young sports clothes, and I don't have to tell you Dana looks her best in formal outfits.'

'Then why involve her at all?' Claudia said, far more calmly than she felt.

'She was threatening to go to London and if she did there was a possibility she would upset Berenice; I can't risk that.'

'Aren't you afraid she'll get fed up with Paris? After all, she has you here.'

'That could happen but I shan't leave her alone for any longer than I can help. She'll be busy with photographers and fittings for the next few days and I'll join her after the show.'

Roman pulled Claudia into his arms and kissed her deeply, taking her by surprise. She pressed closely against him, winding her arms round his neck and opening her mouth in welcome, giving herself up to the desire that flooded through her.

'Claudia, oh, Gemini girl, it's been so long. I was beginning to think you hated me and that I'd never hold you in my arms again,' he said huskily. He ran his hand the length of her spine, making her aware that he wanted her as badly as she wanted him, and for a wild moment she could see no reason why they shouldn't make love. Roman slid the zip of her black cotton dress down to her waist and she shivered as his hand gently explored her smooth shoulder and traced a line from the sensitive pulse in her throat to the valley between her breasts.

'You'll come with me to Paris, Claudia,' he said confidently.

'I want to show you the city that's made for lovers.'

'What about Dana?' Claudia said, stiffening in his arms.

'Forget Dana; she'll be busy with my collection. . .she won't care about us.' Claudia went deathly cold and Roman raised his head, puzzled by the transformation from eager lover into a marble statue.

'Is anything the matter?'

Claudia pulled her dress over her breasts, holding it in place with crossed arms.

'You want me to go to Paris with you as your girlfriend? Where does that leave Dana, or are you going to honour us with your favours on alternate nights?' Roman's eyes narrowed and the colour drained from his face, leaving him cold and withdrawn. He shook his head as if he couldn't believe what he had heard.

'Is that what you think of me? That I intend to make love to both of you?' His anger reached out with a deadly force that made her flinch back from him.

'What else can I think?' she whispered.

'Given your lack of trust in me, nothing.' His
voice lashed like a whip, forcing a cry of pain from
her lips. 'I asked you to trust me but, as that has
proved beyond you, I'll say goodnight.' His eyes,
glittering with rage, bored into hers for one deadly
moment; then he was out of the office before she
could move, and minutes later the showroom door
closed with a precision she knew would remain with
her for a long time.

The next two days passed in a whirl of activity.
Claudia, sleeping hardly at all and eating only when
a worried Myra stood over her, got through them as
best she could. Dana's defection gave her something
to think about apart from Roman, though their last
conversation intruded into everything she did and
invaded her dreams.

She took over the phone in a vain attempt to
replace Dana, only to admit defeat late on Thursday
evening when she was forced, reluctantly, to agree
to Myra's insistence that she wear the wedding gown
herself.

'It makes sense,' Myra said compassionately.

'Yes, I know it does.' Claudia heaved a huge sigh
and tried to smile. 'I just hate the thought of
standing in front of a lot of people.'

'Pretend you're Dana—she loves it,' Myra said
drily. 'I don't want to pry, Claudia, but it doesn't
need a genius to know something went wrong
between you and Roman Wyatt the other night, and
every instinct I have tells me it's something to do
with Dana.' She tilted her head enquiringly.

'Dana is in Paris, working for Roman, and I don't

want to talk about it,' Claudia said bluntly, and with that Myra had to be content. Claudia threw herself into the rehearsal for the show, trying to conquer her nerves by sheer will-power. Roman was never far from her thoughts, and the knowledge that he would be meeting Dana in Paris after the show was very bitter. She went over and over the last time she had seen him. How could he have asked her to go with him when he was going to join Dana?

True, it was one way of keeping Dana from London and a meeting with Berenice, but why go to such lengths? Dana had seemed perfectly happy in Solihull with Roman dancing attention on her every night. Why had her twin gone to Paris, even with the inducement of modelling Roman's finest collection?

Claudia rubbed her hand over eyes that were heavy with tiredness and the tears she refused to shed. She had vowed to fight for Roman's love, but how could she when he only wanted her for a stopgap while Dana was away?

Saturday dawned far too soon. Claudia, waking with a head that felt as if it were filled with lead, almost fell out of bed as her alarm rang. The unhappiness Roman's suggestion had brought, combined with wakeful nights, had made her sleep too heavily.

A shower helped but she still felt languid and disinclined to don the gown she would soon have to wear in front of a discerning audience. Myra greeted her with suppressed excitement and Claudia wished she could feel even a little of the same anticipation. A few weeks ago she would have been looking

forward to the show, but it had all fallen flat and she
had to scold herself severely before she could whip
up any enthusiasm at all.

She sat at her desk and dealt with the post quickly.
There was to be a show in the morning, mainly of
street and casual wear. She wouldn't be required
until the grand finale in the late afternoon, and for
that she gave thanks. She didn't think she could
walk on to the catwalk twice; once was going to take
all the courage she had.

In the evening there was a dinner-dance at the
hotel by the exhibition centre. There had been a
time when she had thought of going with Roman
and dreamed of dancing held tightly in his arms, but
now she doubted she would go at all.

'You must,' Myra said when Claudia said as much
on her return from the hairdresser. 'Your gown will
be the star of the show—you have to go to the
dinner.' Claudia summoned up a smile.

'My gown will be lucky if it gets any attention at
all; you forget some of the top designers are taking
part.'

'None of them can surpass you when it comes to
interpreting a dream,' Myra said loyally, and
Claudia managed to laugh.

'I hope you're right. Now, how do you think my
hair looks?'

'It's perfect—that severe style will suit the dress
and coronet to perfection.' She disappeared to
return immediately with a plate of sandwiches and a
pot of tea. 'You won't have time for a proper meal
but you must eat something—we don't want you
fainting at a crucial moment, do we?' Claudia mur-

mured agreement and ate automatically, though she couldn't taste a thing. The whole world seemed to have lost its flavour since she had fallen in love with a man who didn't love her.

She had just finished drinking her tea when the door opened and Roman came purposefully towards her. Claudia glimpsed Myra's interested face before he closed the door. She jumped to her feet, looking wildly round for escape, but he stood directly between her and the door.

'What do you want?' she demanded in a strained whisper.

'I have to talk to you,' he said hoarsely. 'I haven't been able to sleep or eat since our last meeting and, from the way you look, neither have you,' he said, taking in the discarded food and her too slender form with one glance.

'I thought we'd said everything there was to say,' she said, seeing in her turn the anxious frown and the bleak look in his eyes.

'We said too much and not enough; I can't believe you really think I intend that both you and Dana——' He came to an abrupt halt, and she felt her face grow hot as she remembered the accusation she had flung at him.

'I was angry when I said that. I don't believe you meant. . .' and she, too, allowed her words to die. Roman put his hands on her shoulders.

'That's a relief,' he said, but he didn't sound relieved and she saw the sombre look in his eyes deepen. 'I want you to know the truth, Claudia— that's why I've come, even if it means breaking. . .' Half-finished sentences seemed to be the fashion

today, though it didn't need a crystal ball to finish
this one.

'You promised Dana not to tell me something,'
she said, wondering if he could actually hear her
heart breaking.

'I did, fool that I was, but I didn't intend it to hurt
you so badly.' Claudia winced; it was doubly painful
to have Roman know how much his marriage to
Dana would affect her. She threw up her head
proudly.

'Please don't break your promise to Dana—I shall
survive; and now you must excuse me, I have a lot
to do before I go to the NEC.' She looked straight
into his eyes, seeing a flash of rage at her dismissal.
'Surely you should already be there?'

'I should, but this is more important than a dozen
shows. I want you to listen to me, Claudia.' It was a
command, not a request, and her temper flared.

'I think not; I have no time, even if I would allow
you to tell me something you've promised to keep
secret.'

'It's not like that and you will listen,' he roared.
He reached for her and she stepped nimbly behind a
chair. He tossed it aside as if it were made of straw
and she knew she would be lost if he touched her.
The door opened to reveal a worried-looking Myra.
Roman threw her a look that would melt steel and
she started to withdraw, but Claudia called her to
come in.

'Did you want me, Myra?' she asked as calmly as
if they had been discussing the weather and not
within an ace of making either love or war.

'It's time we left for the NEC,' Myra said, her

eyes darting from Claudia to Roman and back again.
Claudia looked at her watch and exclaimed in shock.

'You're right—what time is the taxi coming?'

'It's here now, but I'll have to follow in another
one—the gown takes up most of the room.'

'Oh, heavens; I hadn't realised that. I wish now I
had sent it on with the rest of the clothes but I didn't
want to risk crushing it.'

'I'm going to the centre—I'll take you, Claudia,
and Myra can look after the gown,' Roman said,
reverting to a competent businessman. Claudia felt
as if she were drowning in a pool of conflicting
emotions; the last thing she wanted was to go
anywhere with Roman and yet the thought of being
with him for a little while longer filled her with
delight.

'That's settled, then,' Myra said happily. 'I'll go
now.' She grinned and hurried away. Claudia
opened her mouth to say she would call a taxi for
herself but one look at the gleam in Roman's amber
eyes changed her mind. She wasn't going to give him
the satisfaction of knowing she dared not be alone
with him for even a few minutes.

She needn't have been afraid; Roman drove
quickly and smoothly, without speaking a word. He
parked the car neatly in the space reserved for
exhibitors and opened the door before she could
release her seatbelt. He held out his hand, and after
a moment's hesitation she put hers into his warm
clasp.

It was a mistake, and she gasped at the intensity
of feeling the slight contact produced. Roman's eyes
narrowed and she knew he was as aware of the

electricity running between them as she was. He pulled her against him, heedless of the interested glances from people getting out of other cars.

'It's still there,' he murmured, and she didn't have to ask what he meant. It was only too evident.

'Roman, not here,' she said frantically as he bent his head and kissed her. He laughed ruefully.

'No, this isn't the place, is it, Gemini girl; you'll be getting a reputation you won't want.' She didn't trust the light in his eyes or the reckles note in his voice. A car horn behind them shattered the air and Roman let her go.

'This discussion is only postponed; we'll talk after the show.' He took her arm and they walked towards the impressive sprawl of the exhibition centre.

'You'll attend the dinner this evening as my partner,' he said, kissing her hard on her mouth as they neared the dressing-room allotted to her. He left swiftly and she gazed after him, the words of refusal unspoken. She turned to the door and it was opened by an anxious Myra.

'Oh, thank goodness. I thought you would never come,' she said as Claudia stepped into a scene of such chaos that it seemed an impossibility they would be ready on time. They were, with minutes to spare, and Claudia, looking at the assembled wedding party, knew her designs had worked. The three bridesmaids, in palest pink, made a picture that complemented the central figure of the bride.

'That dress is perfect on you,' Myra breathed ecstatically. Claudia looked in the long mirror for the last time, and her breath caught in her throat; that beautiful bride couldn't be her.

The gown, in heavy cream satin, followed the curves of her body, flowing to the floor, the princess line only interrupted by a heavy girdle, encrusted with pearl embroidery, slung low on her hips. The medieval line was emphasised by the 'V' of the neck, embroidered to match the girdle, and by the sleeves. They were tight to the elbows then flared out, falling nearly to her knees, allowing the embroidery inside to be seen.

There was a train which repeated the motive of roses and hearts, and a short silk veil flowing, from a circlet of silk roses and pearls, to her shoulders. Instead of flowers she would carry a satin-covered prayerbook with one deep cream rose.

The bridesmaids carried a loop of ribbon and a rose matching their dresses, and Claudia smiled as she saw how effective it all looked. She had elected to keep the group to women only, instead of employing a male model to act as bridegroom, but as she came out of the dressing-room she would have welcomed someone to walk by her side. That someone she would never have; the only man she wanted was beyond her reach and she wouldn't, *couldn't* accept second best, though that was what she would have to do unless she wanted to walk alone forever.

She took a deep breath and stepped from behind the curtains. She had decided in favour of traditional wedding music and a dignified procession. She held her head high as they walked slowly, paused, turned and walked back again.

No one would know how hard it was for her to act the bride she would never be. She neared the exit with relief. Soon her ordeal would be over and she vowed it was the first and last time she would act as model.

A man appeared in the doorway and Claudia's heart missed a beat. She must be dreaming, driven out of her mind by despair. Roman held out his hand as if he was claiming her as his bride and she responded, putting her fingers into his. He bent his head and kissed her, his mouth urgent and seeking, before swinging her up into his arms and carrying her through the curtains.

Applause broke out behind them but she hardly heard a thing. It was heaven to be in Roman's arms, even if he was only playing the part of groom to her bride. What would Dana say if she could see them now? He put her gently on her feet and the click of a door closing made her aware that they were in a small side-room. She turned to him, anger glowing in her blue eyes, and he placed a restraining finger on her lips.

'Before you call me all the names you can think of, and before you demand to know what I think I'm doing, I want to say how lovely you look; your dress is exquisite, but no more than you are. I insist you keep it for yourself—it would be a crime to let anyone else wear it,' he said huskily. Pain shot through her, bleaching all colour from her face. She swayed and Roman caught her to him, exclaiming in dismay.

'What's the matter, Claudia—do you feel ill? It can't have been anything I've said, or can it?' he added as she closed her eyes. He picked her up and sat down on a small settee, keeping his arm round her.

'Don't you mean Dana should keep the dress, Roman? It would be a wicked waste if it isn't worn for its proper purpose.' She tried to stand up but Roman brought his other arm across her, making her his prisoner.

'I agree, and I intend it shall be, but what has Dana got to do with the gown you'll wear for our wedding?'

Claudia opened her eyes wide, unable to believe she had heard him say "our wedding". He was looking at her with such tenderness and love that she thought she would faint from sheer happiness.

'I don't understand,' she said fearfully. 'You're going to Paris to be with Dana and you don't want to get married. You've told me so several times,' she said with a flash of her old spirit. Roman laughed softly.

'I've said a good many foolish things, but that crowns the lot. I not only want to get married but I fully intend to do so as soon as possible, and to you, not to Dana. It has always been you, Gemini girl. From the first moment we met you wove a spell that has bound me to you more securely than chains could ever do.'

'You hated me; you thought I was Garry's lover.'

'I tried to hate you but deep down I knew I was lost and that, however many lovers you'd previously had, I was going to be the last one. Heaven itself opened up for me when we made love and I knew I was the first man in your life. I'm going to be the last,' he warned, a serious note creeping into his voice. Claudia snuggled against him, running her fingers through his hair.

'There could never be anyone else,' she confessed. 'But you still haven't given me any reason why I should marry you.'

'I haven't? Isn't loving you to distraction a good enough reason?' Claudia framed his face between her hands and kissed him softly on his eyes and cheeks before her lips lingered on his mouth.

'That's the first time you've said you love me.'

'It can't be; I must have told you many times before this.' Claudia shook her head, her eyes sparkling with love.

'No, sir; you've said you want me, but no word of love has ever passed your lips.'

'Then I must make up for my error.' His mouth descended on hers in a kiss that reached to the depths of her being. She kissed him back, aware he was as fully aroused as she was. Roman groaned as he tried to push her dress off her shoulders. He ran his fingers down her spine, sighing as he found the zip. Claudia reluctantly stopped him.

'We can't make love here; my dress could be ruined and someone might come in,' she said shyly. She wanted Roman's arms around her, she wanted to feel him against her without the barrier of clothes, but there were things she had to say before she could allow that to happen.

'You're right.' Roman sighed and slid the zip back up and smoothed her crumpled veil. 'I would never forgive myself if I spoilt your gown.' He looked at her shrewdly. 'Your dress and the chance of being interrupted aren't your only reasons for delay, are they, Claudia?'

She shook her head; she could never fool Roman, even for a moment.

'Later, my love,' Roman said briskly and she looked at him in surprise. He smiled, his eyes glowing, and she shivered in anticipation. 'Get out of that dress and we'll go back to your flat—it will be far more comfortable than this dreary room for anything we want to say. . .or do.' He held the door open for her and escorted her back to the dressing-room.

'Hurry,' he said simply. 'I'll be waiting.' Claudia dressed in her own clothes, a dazed expression on her face that effectively silenced the questions Myra wanted to ask. She smiled vaguely when Myra asked her about the dinner and walked out of the room into Roman's waiting arms.

He kissed her and hurried her out of the building and into his car. Myra watched them go, a happy smile on her face, before she turned back into the dressing-room to swathe the wedding gown in its covers. It would certainly be needed, and very soon, if she could read the signs.

Roman helped Claudia out of the car when they reached her flat, took the key from her and opened the door.

'I'll put the kettle on,' Claudia said; she wanted something to do—it was silly to feel shy, but there was something between them today that made the very air vibrate.

'Later,' he said again. He pushed her gently down on to the settee and sat so close to her that she could hardly breathe for fear that she'd betray how much she wanted him.

'I want to make love to you more than anything in the world, but you have doubts about me and I want everything crystal-clear between us, so ask your questions, Gemini girl.' She drew back from him and took him at his word.

'Where does Dana come into all this? You're supposed to be meeting her in Paris tomorrow, aren't you?'

Roman shook his head. 'Not any longer.' He took a letter from his pocket and held it out to her. 'Dana sent you this enclosed in a letter to me, but before you open it I want you to know that Dana means no more to me than a rather troublesome sister-in-law-to-be. I've never thought of her in any other way and never will; she may look like you, physically, but inside you're as different as you can possibly be. You are unselfish and care for other people more than for yourself; you're also outstanding and original in what you do.

'You are the positive side of the Gemini character, while Dana is the negative.'

Claudia looked at him in astonishment. 'I thought you didn't believe in star signs?'

Roman laughed ruefully. 'I didn't until I met you, but loving you made me want to know how twins could be so different. You do know Gemini is a dual sign?'

'So is Sagittarius—half-man, half-horse,' Claudia teased.

'The two signs complement each other, but you are the twin I want, not Dana.'

'Then why did you dance attendance on her?' Claudia demanded, her resentment bursting the bonds she had placed upon it. Roman held her closely to him and rested his face against hers.

'I've hurt you badly, Claudia, but no more than I've hurt myself. It was necessary if I was to prevent Dana rushing up to London and ruining any chance of a reconciliation between Berenice and Garry, to say nothing of the risk to the baby. Dana threatened to do just that if I didn't "dance attendance"; Garry is easily swayed and still half in love with Dana—I dare not risk it.' He grimaced as if he had a bad taste in his mouth.

'It was the last thing I wanted to do, but everything was in the balance. Dana continually hinted that she would take off for London if I refused to do just what she wanted, or if I said anything to you. I could have strangled her many times; only the fact that she's your sister prevented me.'

Claudia, shocked that Dana could resort to blackmail, touched his face gently and opened her letter. It was very short. She read it twice and passed it over to Roman.

'Dana is very sorry for all the trouble she has caused and wants me to forgive her.'

'You will, of course,' Roman said, replacing the note in the envelope.

'She's all the family I have, and I'm sure she means it. She also says she loves Paris and intends to stay there. I wonder how long it will be before she gets tired of working there?' A smile spread over Roman's face.

'It could be a lifetime.' He laughed at Claudia's startled expression. 'The letter your note came in was from Pierre Labone,' he said, naming one of

France's top designers. 'Pierre is my partner in Paris; he's a very wealthy and handsome man. He's also young and single, strong-minded, and very taken with your sister. I think he will make sure she stays in France.

'Pierre is a Leo—he should be able to keep your wayward sister in order.'

Claudia laughed.'You *have* gone into astrology, haven't you? Oh, Roman, I'm so pleased for Dana. I know she can be difficult, but she is my sister and I love her.'

'We can visit them—after we're married, not before. I won't risk Pierre seeing you until you're my wife. You will marry me, Claudia?'

'Is that an order or a question?' she asked, the mischievous light in her eyes fading as she saw the anxiety mirrored in his. 'Yes, I will marry you; you know I will.'

Roman's lips sought hers passionately and she held nothing back. The kiss lengthened until he groaned and lifted his head.

'The sooner we're married, the better. I want to make love to you for days and days, not to mention the nights,' he added with a wicked twinkle in his eyes. He got up, drawing her with him.

'I've got a special licence in my pocket; if I'd been obliged to go to Paris you'd have come with me as my wife.' Claudia looked at him, her love shining in her eyes.

'I like your programme,' she said softly, 'but there's just one thing wrong with it.'

'What's that?' Roman asked, a wary look in his eyes.

'The time factor; it's too late to get married today, but the honeymoon doesn't have to wait, does it?' she said, a faint colour stealing into her face as he swung her into his arms.

'I hoped you'd say that—why do you think I brought you here, where we can be alone?'

'For a rehearsal, what else?' Claudia said demurely as Roman carried her into the bedroom.

STARGAZING

YOUR STAR SIGN: **GEMINI (May 21–June 20)**

GEMINI is the third sign of the Zodiac, ruled by the planet Mercury and controlled by the element Air. These make you inquisitive, witty, cheerful and—sometimes—inconsistent. Renowned for your dual personality, you tend to be fickle, but being a creature of the moment could be an advantage as you may make note of something today and make it tomorrow's aim!

Socially, Geminis are friendly and natural communicators—you love to chat with people about anything, just to find out what makes them tick. Even though you are a social butterfly and a gracious host, your moody side see permanence at home restrictive—so your family might have to wait a while for the dust to settle!

Your characteristics in love: restless and spirited, Gemini do not like to be tied down and partners may find them unreliable, since they are considered to be born flirts. Your twin nature allows you to handle many things at the same time—and that includes lovers! Nevertheless, you are quick-minded and can talk yourself out of trouble so that partners are left exhausted by trying to keep up with you!

Signs which are compatible with you: **Leo**, **Aries**, **Libra** and **Aquarius**, while **Taurus**, **Virgo** and **Scorpio** provide you with a challenge. Partners born under other signs can be compatible, depending on which planets reside in their Houses of Personality and Romance.

What is your star-career? Able to juggle many things in the air at once, Geminis enjoy a great deal of variety in their work. Employment which involves good communication skills and versatility will attract you, such as publishing, broadcasting, interpreting, teaching and counselling.

Your colours and birthstones: Your favourite colours are bright blue and yellow which are sometimes combined in interiors. Your birthstones are agate; a mutable stone found in different colours reflecting the chameleon-like nature of this mercurial sign and pearl, a rare gem which is regarded as a symbol of chastity and purity.

GEMINI ASTRO-FACTFILE

Day of the week: Wednesday
Countries: United States and Wales
Flowers: Lily of the valley, lavender and rose
Food: Chicken and shrimps; Gemini cook on the spur of the moment, often trying unusual or exotic food since variety is the spice of life!
Health: Make sure your nervous energy does not exhaust your body as basic body functions such as eating and sleeping are just as important. Learn to relax more by breathing correctly and treating tension with a massage!

You share your star sign with these famous names:

Paul McCartney   Kylie Minogue
Bob Hope   Cilla Black
Clint Eastwood   Joan Collins
Mike Gatting   Priscilla Presley
Bob Dylan   Kathleen Turner

Next Month's Romances

Each month you can choose from a world of variety in romance with Mills & Boon. Below are the new titles to look out for next month, why not ask either Mills & Boon Reader Service or your Newsagent to reserve you a copy of the titles you want to buy — just tick the titles you would like to order and either post to Reader Service or take it to any Newsagent and ask them to order your books.

Please save me the following titles:	Please tick	√
DARK RANSOM	Sara Craven	
TAKEN BY STORM	Sandra Field	
LESSON TO LEARN	Penny Jordan	
WALK UPON THE WIND	Patricia Wilson	
WHIRLPOOL	Madeleine Ker	
COERCION TO LOVE	Michelle Reid	
LOVE RULES	Ann Charlton	
HIDDEN MEMORIES	Vanessa Grant	
MAID FOR MARRIAGE	Sue Peters *(Faraway Places)*	
THE SINGING TREE	Anne Weale	
LOVE IS A RISK	Jennifer Taylor	
MIRACLES CAN HAPPEN	Stephanie Howard *(Starsign)*	
BLOSSOMING LOVE	Deborah Davis	
STRONG MAGIC	Christine Greig	
THE STORY PRINCESS	Rebecca Winters	
GOBLIN COURT	Sophie Weston	

If you would like to order these books from Mills & Boon Reader Service please send £1.70 per title to: Mills & Boon Reader Service, P.O. Box 236, Croydon, Surrey, CR9 3RU and quote your Subscriber No:..(If applicable) and complete the name and address details below. Alternatively, these books are available from many local Newsagents including W.H.Smith, J.Menzies, Martins and other paperback stockists from 8th June 1992.

Name:..

Address:..

....Post Code:........................

To Retailer: If you would like to stock M&B books please contact your regular book/magazine wholesaler for details.

You may be mailed with offers from other reputable companies as a result of this application.
If you would rather not take advantage of these opportunities please tick box ☐